The Sinister Affair
of the Blue Men

This book is dedicated to the sea and those who sail her.

Table of Contents

1.

The Signalman's Calling

Brazen words fell off the tongue of the Flag Captain, as the young and focused Lieutenant Blackmarsh drank in their import. His ears were pricked keenly to record every detail, shade, or hue of nuance that could be teased from the officer's report. As the situation of the war with Napoleon had become even murkier with his recent encroachments towards the Kingdom of Denmark and Norway; and recent intelligence intercepted by British spies in Copenhagen of the French request to Russia to a combined alliance of naval powers to include the Danish-Norwegian fleet; all the factors suggested the growing danger towards the British fleet. To add to this political turmoil- which was near to boiling over- during the summer of 1807, several cargo ships laden with grain and other foodstuffs had vanished, while still more had re-appeared, abandoned, on the rocky shores of the Outer Hebrides.

It was the opinion of the Admiralty, in the personage of Admiral Lord Gambier, and his esteemed colleague General Arthur Wellesley- later known as the 1st Duke of Wellington- that the missing crew, and their vessels, may be as a result of piratical activity by rogue brigantines belonging to the Dano-Norwegian fleet. The moment for some clarity had now burgeoned to the highest import, and when the Admiral requested a competent officer to investigate the matter, Wellesley recommended Lieutenant Jeremiah Anthony Blackmarsh of his signals officer service. This very same youth had verily proved himself a keen Kentish man, himself, hailing from Blackheath, who had several times stolen the thunder of his own superiors in solving oddities at regiment. He was adept at the use of both the Murray Lettered Telegraph, and the Radiated Telegraph System, and was appraised of all telegraph flags of the Admiralty to boot.

Under these orders and backdrop, Lt. Blackmarsh learned of his transfer to Scotland: to observe the area; to investigate the causes for the mystery of the lost crews and ships; and by all means to put and end to the business. The junior officer had, at last, received his first greatly-yearned official calling!

***

Blackmarsh, a portly man for his years, had prepared for his journey north by sequestering funds from regiment and a modest travel pack of goods, and food, to aid his progress on his wayward assignment. As the mission he had been tasked for was a delicate one, he had been issued permission to travel incognito to avoid raising the suspicion and the dander of possible foreign agents on the route. In many ways Jeremiah saw himself in search of the clew- that ball of string- which Ariadne had given Theseus to escape the maze of the Minotaur of Greek mythology. He, too, would need to find "a tangible" to blow off the sea's brume, illuminating the mystery of the ships. What could this be, he had puzzled inwardly, as he made his way by carriage northward?

Instructions given by Flag Captain Lattimer were that Blackmarsh could expect to make his way up the backbone of England from fort to fort, changing horses at each, until he made it to the Scottish border. From thence, he would acquire local transport, for which end the funds, he carried sewn into the hem of his bodice. On his person, the Lieutenant held a written order from the Admiralty informing His Majesty's military officials to effect his quick transfer and provide him with aid towards his confidential mission, without substantial delay. This was folded into a small square of thick parchment bearing the seal of the Admiralty.

Being a portly bespectacled, odd, and tallish Kentish man, this small square would certainly provide a fascinating lever for the out-of-place fellow, to tug the eye of any person who beheld the letter, causing a quite involuntary and jerky raising of the eyebrow. The ego of the young man was helplessly held captive to the novelty of unfurling this revelation at each successive turn, once presented with the necessity, enabling him to de-pocket it from the secret inner bodice-pocket of his clothing. Jeremiah saw that this letter held a powerful sway over his ability to command and cause obeisance, which upon deeper consideration of the matter, he decided, subsequently, to limit its use, whenever his own powers of persuasion could supplant the letter's application. The idea smacked, for one, of a very French fashion- begging to follow the likes of the absolute monarch, Louis XIV, of France. This was a personage- an autocrat- which Blackmarsh sternly wished to avoid emulating; especially now that similarly, if not worse, that absolute tyrant and Emperor of France, Bonaparte, was viewed effectively as the principle adversary to his own nation. Jeremiah's own morality was blooming and he had arrived at his own sensible rationale for the employment of power and force in his role of a secret signals officer to the Crown. During his service he should always strive to remain a red-coat, as opposed to the Napoleonic blue-coats!

After passing through Carlisle and its garrison, through the last of Cumberland, Jeremiah Anthony made his way on to Dumfries to rest at an inn and procure fresh intelligence in Scotland. While traversing the territory, the junior officer was astonished by the outcropping remnants of Hadrian's Wall, still visibly jutting through the bracing landscape of the North. This remnant bespoke tales of ancient visitors to this land- conquerors no less- that had brought the chains of their Mediterranean masters to Britain in the days of Caesar. Would the upstart Buonaparte enjoy the same success in the coming times, pondered Blackmarsh in bitter worry? He had certainly hoped it would not to come to pass; yet, in the view of the Navy, he had been sent roving, to play his own hand, ensuring that this not happen, should the French or their allies be behind the plundered merchant vessels. Jeremiah Anthony paused for a moment. Plundered? Not as such! The facts relayed by Flag Captain Lattimer mentioned nothing specifically of the sort. His brazen words had raised the picture of a specter at work. Crews had vanished, as well as some few ships, yet no specific detail of ballast being stolen or otherwise disposed of was addressed in his report. This bespoke an agency of uncertain surprise. Had the crews been impressed into the navy of the pirates? Had the other vessels been captured or scuppered? Many key instances were under-reported in the Flag Captain's report. Blackmarsh's conclusion was that Headquarters simply had not a clue whence these had disappeared. The young man picked up his journey and continued towards his destination of Dumfries. The green Lieutenant had never in his life been to Scotland, nor had he even dreamed that he would be roused to that legendary location of cold winds and time-weathered legends of old.

On the path leading in to the city, Blackmarsh was met by a local man who addressed him in an oddly familiar, yet friendly manner.

"Yer cuddy bee a draggin a wee; I see yer naut fromm theise parts, laddie!" spoke the stranger.

"Pardon?" responded Jeremiah… "cuddy?"

"Aye, man! Yer horse! It's lookin peekèd an all! Have ye watered thot nag?" he retorted in explaining his gist.

"Yes! Certainly so! She's an old mare, you know." said Anthony relieved to grasp his meaning.

"Bee ye passin thruw ar stoppin in Dumfries?"

"I should like a room for the night. Can you suggest a place at a fair price? I have merchant affairs to attend in the area." said the Lieutenant.

"Well, ay shan't tell a fyb, bat ol' MacTavish's inn is fayr and his missus makes a bonnie haggis!"

"Where be this then; sorry, your name was..?"

"Jock. Jock Cotts is ay! Yue take dat rode ther an turn left whyn ye sees thot muckle whaite haus, then ye bee in the spot- an giv thot cuddy a gud drink!"

"Yes, many thanks to you Jock Cotts. That I aim to do!"

Soon the figure of the local man Cotts had vanished from the horizon as the stout Lieutenant made his route directly to the inn of the MacTavishes. A laconic wooden sign reading "Inn" hung from the large white house, which dominated the main thoroughfare of the town. Jeremiah tied his old mare to a hitch and walked into the building, as no-one was lingering outside the place. He was promptly intercepted by a man and a lady inside, who were engaged in what sounded like village gossiping. The pair were both aged in their forties and had the look of country rustics, if Blackmarsh had ever spied a rustic.

"Master MacTavish, I presume?" spoke the young man.

The two immediately burst into a peel of raucous laughter, after the junior officer's pronouncement of the syllables. Blackmarsh's face assumed a pinkish red tint of flush, as he was overcome by embarrassment.

"I beg your pardon?" he retorted, "Have I offended thee?"

"Nay, nay, forgive us, good gentleman! You've been having a chin wag with old Jock Cotts, I am to suppose!" said the man in perfect English.

"Yes, how could you possibly divine that?" said Anthony in surprise.

"That Jock is quite a merryman! He plays that game with every Sacsannach coming into town! We are the Ainsleys. MacTavish and his wife have been dead for nigh on twenty years! I don't know why he does it, but brings us our trade at any rate."

"Most unorthodox, yet, you seem to be blessed with a roaming mountebank to draw in your lodgers, all the same. *Sacsannach-* Englishman?" replied a slightly confused Jeremiah Anthony.

"Yes and yes- true on both scores. We, are also 'Sacsannachs.' We hail from Cumberland, but came up here and took up this inn after the MacTavishes perished of the cholera and palsy."

"Do you still serve the legendary haggis?" inquired the Lieutenant, with a look of hunger in his eyes.

"That we do- with neepes and a dram of whiskey!" replied the innkeeper.

"I should command to dine soonest, and without a doubt take on a room overhead. Can you water my cuddy?"

"All's well under this roof. Please, make yourself easy, I'll show you your bonnie billet." said the innkeep, glad at the young man's apparition.

Blackmarsh turned his head as he prodded up the stairs to notice that the lady had already fetched a wooden bucket with water for his horse outside. He, too, looked forward to a hardy rustic meal in the quaint, yet, busy market-town. Once alone in his billet, Blackmarsh inspected the gear he had acquired for his mission- his collapsible brass Royal Navy telescope was in fine condition, being no less the wear of the bumpy journey from the regiment hence. It was still snug in its case. A map of the western Scottish coast was tucked into his large pocket in the bodice; in addition, the bodice secreted three golden George III Half-Guinea coins and a number of shillings and pence; a small sketchbook and a pencil filled a small belt-pouch at his side; and lastly, secured within his left legging, a Bristol made razor for shaving. Apart from these, the young Lieutenant was wholly without weaponry for fear of raising suspicion on his journey. Blackmarsh tidied his belongings in order and went downstairs after hearing the urging of the lady Ainsley calling him to table.

At table, Blackmarsh was treated to an impressive portion of victuals, which he imagined that even the spartan Ainsleys, themselves, hadn't likely eaten so grandly. The haggis, a new dish for him, was foreign to his palate, yet, savory and was united cleverly with the mashed neepes and whiskey refreshment. After the meal was downed with relish, the curious traveler attempted to engage the innkeeper and his wife on news of the area of possible interest. Alas, they had not heard anything "worth the telling," according to the proprietor. He did, however, earnestly suggest that Blackmarsh, should he want to discover news of the area, consult with *The Dumfries Weekly Journal,* which would be published on the morrow, should he be so inclined.

Jeremiah Anthony had not considered the possibility of reading in the press about the local happenings, but decided he would do just that, taking the innkeep at his suggestion. He inquired, as to the cuddy's lodging, only to be reassured by the "missus," in the parlance of Jock Cotts, that the old mare had been stowed out back under roof and shelter, while the Lieutenant had unpacked his stocks. Satisfied that the journey had progressed well, Blackmarsh opted for bedding down early so that he would be full of vigor on the morrow for an auspicious and early rise. The stout Lieutenant returned to his billet, made ready for bed, and lastly removed his spectacles, placing them on the night table adjacent his rope bed.

The junior officer awoke in anguishing pain on the morrow. Attempting to put his full girth on his legs, he strained in vain. A night's sleep on the rope-strung bed of the inn had put a severe crook into his back that resisted his efforts at rising. He paused to recover the stamina he required and finally wrenched himself into an upright position. After dressing, a laborious and punishingly relentless task, the young officer languished downward into the common-room of the inn, where a hash and salted-ham breakfast awaited him.

"You look the worse for it, young fella!" said the innkeep.

"The meat of my back seems to have had an argument with your berth. I take it the berth was the victor!" smirked Jeremiah Anthony.

"I should not care to gainsay that, my fine fellow! I've got the eyes in my head, you see!" said the innkeep, joining his wife in laughing at the pronouncement of their pained guest.

"I took the liberty to get you the tidings, as I went over to exchange words with a good chum of mine." explained the innkeep. He handed Jeremiah the news of Dumfries.

The young man pulled it towards himself to peruse it briefly, but was halted by the "missus." "But mind you finish your meal first, young fella!" intoned the hostess.

Jeremiah, not wanting to appear ogreish, opted for the diplomatic resolution, and agreed with her considerable thoughtfulness on the topic. The hash went down well, with a large tankard filled with local ale, with which he whetted his palate. The rush to devour the meal was belabored by the young Lieutenant's wish to avoid even the slightest scandal or row while on the mission. One never knows, he thought to himself, from which vector a sought-after morsel of intelligence may be rendered. Certainly the Ainsleys were steeped in their lore of the area, and as prodigious gossipers, would have purchase over a significant stratum of regional information, local personalities, surprising incidences, and down-right libelous accusations and rumors of nearly anything worth knowing in these parts.

Blackmarsh analyzed his options. If he inquired about the loss of the shipping, this could cast the light of wonder on the locals, yet, at some point in time, this Rubicon would need to be crossed. He was still not quite sure whether the couple could be trusted and taken into confidence. It was at this vantage that he reckoned he had traipsed into this northern-most zone, without having prepared a suitable masquerade or fig-leaf, from behind which he could hide his genuine reason for the voyage. Beyond the meager veil of "on merchant business," he had not concocted a detailed story to explain his affair in the area. This he deemed essential to conceive prior to delving any deeper into the Scottish hinterlands, without the benefit of cover.

The meal was, at last, fully masticated, and only an empty plate confronted the young signalman, for which he graciously thanked the couple, and complemented the lady on her mastery of the culinary arts. This whisper of praise brought a sea of red blush to her stout round cheeks. Smelling the occasion to vacate the common-room, Blackmarsh begged his pardon and quickly trotted back to his billet, where he could see by the light of his glass-paned window to read.

The paper was perfectly crammed with all varieties of sundry advertisement for the buying and selling of merchandise, yet there was also a significant amount of local gossip being traded in the newspaper. J.A. perused the various columns and sheets of the publication searching for anything of remote interest to his research. Suddenly, his eyes bulged as they met a small section on the paper's penultimate page. A neutral Danish vessel, "The Otter," had called at the Stevenson brothers' whiskey distillery in the sparsely-populated settlement referred to as Oban, to take on barrels!

Blackmarsh swallowed hard as his breakfast threatened to come back up. Had he found his first clew, in this Scottish labyrinth?

2.

To the Firth of Lorne

An Linne Latharnach- The Firth of Lorne, as Jeremiah Anthony was told by a villager, was the Gaelic appellation for his newest clew in the mystery of the ships. He, thus, prepared to make the arrangements for a swift sea voyage to Oban. After much questioning of the host and hostess, as to the best way to reach the sea, Blackmarsh was appraised of two nearly equal routes to the Firth of Clyde on the sea. The first variant would take him north over land to Ayr. The second variant involved an equal distance over dry land to the western jutting peninsula, terminating at Portpatrick. Both port cities offered the possibility to engage a fishing vessel for carriage over the waves towards Oban, and the Firth of Lorne. Blackmarsh poured over his map of the western coast of Scotland, which dominated his fixed gaze.

Two notations hung in the Lieutenants mind. Whereas Ayr, an old fishing village, was more and more finding itself as a resort destination, there would be the risk of a larger swathe of society, perhaps even foreign spies present. This caused Jeremiah to balk at the prospect. The other notation hanging in his postulating mind was, with the selection of Portpatrick, there was a greater chance of Royal Navy vessels harbored. If he had experienced an ill pickle in taking on a craft to Oban, the option of commandeering a military vessel remained open. If he choose this path, the speed of the vessel, too, would not hinder his mission, such as would in the case of a slower merchant craft or fishing boat. The job he had been saddled with was, indeed, of highest importance to the Admiralty. He, therefore, had settled the matter in his mind. The arguments for Portpatrick were weightier than those for Ayr. As the day was still young, the Lieutenant folded up his map, went downstairs, paid for all the services rendered by the Ainsleys, and took, Maggie, the old mare by the reins. He started down the road to Portpatrick. After twenty odd miles, and the warmth of the July sun baking the two, Maggie faltered on the road. Jeremiah dismounted to steady the poor beast, who was clearly poorly. He open his water-skin with cool drink, which he decanted into his palm for the horse to taste, but his gesture was too late. She perspired on the spot, just outside of the village of Twynholm.

The young officer felt a tinge of panic burgeoning in his bosom. What would he do now? Stranded in the countryside, in a foreign place, he would have to think fast. He debated whether he should remain with the animal or push on. After a few moments of pondering the matter, Blackmarsh stomached the animal's passing, but decided to head into the village and request help from a villager. He set off into the village, which was less than a mile off.

The place was a quaint little sleepy hamlet, and J.A. soon located a pub and inn in the center. He navigated towards the pub, which appealed to him, as he was starting to feel the rigors of the voyage. Walking into the small establishment, he peered around and noticed only four patrons having ale and murmuring quietly. Once at the bar, not wanting to be a bore, Blackmarsh ordered a small beer and a dram of whiskey. He paid the owner, and downed the whiskey as the sweat of his labors roiled off his forehead.

"Therr bee nae danger in speekin of yer problem, chum." said a patron.

Blackmarsh spun around to view his interlocutor. It was, by the Lieutenants reckoning, a farmer or laborer.

"Yes! Quite. My cuddy, that poor soul, dropped off on the road here. Died, she did, on me. I require a burial for her." he explained.

"There'z a fyne chum! A gravedigger bee me! Gavin Morr at yer servis! Mind ye, the servis t'aint withaut cost." replied the middle-aged man.

"Would three shillings suffice, Master Gavin? I mean for a proper burial mind you." inquired the signals officer.

"Dun and dun!" exclaimed the digger. "You shew them coin and drink upp. Whaile ye drinks, ay'll be a diggin. Wher does the bonnie lay noo?"

"At present, just to the east there yonder, nigh on a mile outside the hamlet. Much obliged, Master Morr!"

Jeremiah Anthony watched the man quaff the dregs of his brew and he hurried back the same road he himself had prior traversed. Out of the window, he spied the digger retrieve a spade from the roadside, that he had secreted while calling at the public house. The owner of the establishment queried the young traveler about his business and reason for calling. Blackmarsh puzzled for a moment before replying. He had still not come up with a masquerade of his mission to explain his northern rovings. Words of creative inspiration fell from the mouth of the portly junior officer.

"Its the merchant trade, you know. Was on my way to Portpatrick to hire a sea-craft. I have business up north on the coast." he embellished ad libitum.

"Whay Portpatrick? It bee far. Gatehouse of Fleet bee jost seven miles down this road. There bee plenty o' craft to hyre thence!" corrected the man.

"Ah. Yes, I could call there, it just as good for me. Your counsel is most profitable. Much obliged, my good fellow!" said the flummoxed Jeremiah.

Not wanting to outstay the good cheer of the locals, Blackmarsh, downed the last of his ale and returned the empty tankard to the table, where he had taken a seat. He dropped a coin on to the table, payment for the helpful advice of the owner, and asked that the three remaining coins, which he stacked forming a small tower, be presented to Gavin Morr, when he returned from his mortuary errand. After a nod from the proprietor, the stout officer departed with a small stagger in his step. Clearly the local fire-water was having an effect on his gait. As he walked into the heart of the hamlet, J.A. glanced to and fro, searching for a horse and carriage to hire for the road to Gatehouse of Fleet.

After a quarter hour of searching the sparely populated village, he was passed on the road by a wagon with a pair of sailors, seated in the back compartment.

"Good Sir!" shrieked the Lieutenant.

The driver slowed and finally came to a halt. Blackmarsh ran up to the man, evidently a farmer, and inquired if he had room for a passenger to Gatehouse of Fleet.

"Och aye! Headid ther noo! Hop upp lad; t'aint no quandary fir mee!" said the man.

Jeremiah Anthony did as much and chatted with the sailors on the way to port. From these he learned that the farmer was a father to one of the sailors. They were both headed there to board their vessel, the HMS Panther. This news filled the Lieutenant with a sudden brain-brat. He prodded the sailors with queries about the Panther's next port of call, and asked what kind of vessel she was. According to the youngest man, who was a mate to the Boatswain, the ship was a "glorious vessel" and an "Edgar Class ship of the line," with a double deck and sixty canon on board. Most impressive, thought Blackmarsh. The mate explained that the ship was due for Plymouth, where she would be refitted to serve as a prison hulk for transporting convicts.

Jeremiah's mind was flooded by a deluge of prospects. Would he be able to commandeer the vessel for his mission? If this truly were the last voyage of the Panther, what captain would not resist a last dramatic jaunt up the Scottish coast, through the firths, to convey a secret delegate from the Admiralty? It was worth a try. Jeremiah still had adequate funds in his bodice, yet, the speed at which he could advance his mission was too tempting. The mystery of the ships haunted him with a scarcity of facts. He needed to make progress soonest! At stake was potentially the fleet itself, reasoned the signals officer. Yes. He would unleash "the order" once more for this reason. It was a measured decision, tempered with the urgency of his errand.

***

Lt. Jeremiah Anthony Blackmarsh stood on the deck of the HMS Panther in the company of the Boatswain and his mate, the sailor who had accompanied the signals officer to town, and then in a row-boat to the high masted, double-decked HMS Panther. The vessel's commander, Captain Davis, had been summoned to the quarterdeck to receive the odd visitor. The stern-looking captain, a man of approximately fifty years age, with a prominent tuft of gray hair curling about his forehead like a great octopus upon an under-water rock, approached the junior officer and took to hand the folded orders handed over by Blackmarsh.

"The Admiralty." announced the Boatswain, whose intonation peaked at the word's penultimate syllable.

Naturally, such a sudden and unexpected pronouncement caused the senior officer's eyebrow to arch upward, forming the shape of a curled sea shrimp. Davis unfolded the parchment, combing the written lines with his piercing orbs. A sublime grin began to form across the man's bronzed cheeks, spanning out slowly in opposite directions. He addressed the men.

"Boatswain raise the anchor! Helmsman, prepare your course for...., excuse me, Sir...?"

"Lt. Blackmarsh. Your destination is Oban, in the Firth of Lorne." he replied succinctly.

"Oban, in the Firth of Lorne!" he parroted up to the helm.

"Don't rightly now what your affair is, Lt. Blackmarsh, but this ship is headed to its doom. I'm only too happy to forestall that eventuality, therefore your presence here is as a boon! One last bound of glory for the Panther, before she be turned into a damnable scow for convicts."

"The honor, Commander, is all mine! I've noticed you're flying the Blue Ensign. Is it for the vessel's decommission?"

"Quite so. As we sailed into port for our last call before Plymouth, we ceased flying the Red Ensign. This ship has been made ready to meet her doom!" caustically commented the Commander.

"I've some training in the signal flags; may I view the Panther's bunting and their stowage?" requested Anthony.

"Boatswain! Take this gentleman to the bunts, and let him have a good look!" intoned the Captain obligingly.

As the vessel's captain strode off to see to the navigation, Blackmarsh was given a thorough presentation of the signal flags in current usage by the Navy, and was verily impressed. Though these flags had seen, winds, rains, and gales aplenty, the collection fascinated the young Jeremiah; to imagine an entire veritable language was contained in these! It had been some time since he had observed the full stock of signal flags in Navy usage. What was it that Admiral Horatio Nelson had signaled before the battle of Trafalgar, pondered Blackmarsh? Examining the flags present he pieced the message together. The Boatswain stared in miscomprehension at the script in flags. At that instant the signalman appeared and mouthed the sending.

"*'England expects that every man will do his duty.'* Who's having a laugh then? Do we have a Nelson on deck?" cried the man in be-wonderment.

"I still have it!" shrieked Anthony, glad that his knowledge was still "topping," as they saying goes.

After the laughter resided, the Boatswain showed their guest to his quarters, next to Captain Davis' quarters. So, apparently the 1st Mate had surrendered his berth without a peep, as if a mere symbolic white flag was hoisted in his absence. The Lieutenant stretched out for a kip in the mate's hammock of this, his temporary quarters, only to be roused by a mate, who brought in the visitor's sea rations. These were quite drab, consisting of- a mush of peas; a small morsel of pickled cod, topped with a slice of lime; and lastly a drinking cup filled with a fishy smelling ale. Blackmarsh took these foodstuffs into custody, and despite the poor quality of the catch, made quick work of the lot, downing them in the blink of an eye. He hadn't properly eaten since he had left Dumfries, in fact!

After the meal had been dispensed with unceremoniously, Jeremiah Anthony set his mind to concocting a believable story for his journey to the distillery in Oban. It must, to use a nautical term, be absolutely water-tight, he mused to himself. He still essentially had a mystery on his hands. Was the disappearances of the crews an example of impressment into foreign navies by pirates? What of the ships? It is odd that some ships had gone missing, yet others ended up on the rocks. He wondered to himself, had these too drifted, only, instead of hitting land, merely drifted out into the North Atlantic? It was a possibility. Yet, the cause of so many vessels suffering this fate, perhaps five or six to his understanding, was a colossal blow to the mercantile trade. That none of these had been warships, "ships of the line," so to speak, did rather speak loudly to the signals officer. Was it merely chance that such a foe would not easily be lured into any trap, rendering itself a nut proving much more difficult to crack? It could be happenstance, as well. Jeremiah considered these angles, whilst his mind changed tack.

J.A. returned to the task of subterfuge; that of concocting his cover. If he was charged with a scientific mission, say, the mapping of the coast, it could be more believable. As a merchant trader, he had come with no wares to trade, nor did he have the knowledge of the trade, to any degree of perfection, to pass himself off as such. Trading terms were foreign and wholly unknown to him. Yet with the blanket cartography excuse, he could very well have been employed by a company to survey the optimum route for transit of specific wares, and suggest the route for use in navigation. Perhaps a new route across the sea to Canada? He could chance this explanation, if needed, without explaining too much. It would also bring him into contact with the seafarers and fishermen of the Scottish coast. He would be in a prime position to assess the threat and danger of enemy or other activity, surely, via the lore and knowledge of these folk. As he turned these points over in his head, the stout Lieutenant became drowsy, and before the night had fallen, was out like an extinguishing candle stub.

***

Jeremiah Anthony Blackmarsh wormed in his hammock. Although he had managed to get some shut-eye, he was awoken in the early morning hours by the ebb and flow of the waves, as the vessel moved through the waves in the North Channel, well outside of the Firth of Clyde. They had been sailing in the open seas, and the junior officer had not known of the pleasures of such an experience prior. The thought of the fishy tankard of ale, sat poorly with the seas-sickened man, while he attempted to stave off the heaves. During the night, he awoke once, as he heard the captain dictate the vessel's speed, which he appraised at six knots. Ground-fall was not to be expected before a full day and a half voyage had been undertaken. This meant another sleepless night for Blackmarsh. He certainly hoped by then that he should have sprouted his long-awaited sea-legs. At the crack of dawn, to cap off the horrid quality of rest obtained, the rotund undercover man was blasted out of his berth by a barrel-man in the crow's nest, rousing the crew to general quarters. Jeremiah Anthony scrambled up on deck and retracted his telescope. He fixed his gaze to starboard, as were several other officer's from the poop deck.

The morning sun had peeked over the horizon to reveal two vessels in close formation, hugging the other, as they moved northeasterly. The navigator held his sextant firmly and made calculations on their position.

"Ten to twelve miles out. North by northwesterly course. Flying a red ensign with white cross!" he bellowed back to the 1st Mate.

Blackmarsh couldn't see the coloration in his weaker scope, but could detect the blurry outline of the two hulks. At this distance, they had to be warships. Red ensign with white cross! Jeremiah Anthony's heart pumped rapidly in his chest. They had spotted two Danish ships of the line! The commander ordered the ship to bank hard to port and steer the vessel into the channel, with the Isle of Islay on their port and Colonsay Isle on their starboard. The had just entered the southernmost islands of the Inner Hebrides. At the end of this channel, they would find Oban. With a good ten hours of sailing, they would make their destination before nightfall. The two Danish ships, technically neutral, stayed out of range and appeared to ignore their presence altogether. Had they eluded the gaze of the other ships or had their presence actually been spotted, to be recorded in their logbooks?

Only time would tell what had come to pass, yet Blackmarsh teemed with exuberance. After steadying himself, he had gained his sea-legs, and was looking forward to a hearty breakfast on board HMS Panther. Sailing into the channel was a relief to all. Jeremiah Anthony took pleasure in another standard meal, such as the day before, however, the fishy ale was gracefully replaced by a cup of sweet Jamaican rum. The victuals were attacked with all the gusto of a starving young signalman, who had by his count, missed several unfortunate meals! Once on dry land, he would remedy this with a crusty sandwich of roast beef, if he was able to scout one out, he placated himself.

By midday the ship was already navigating the waters of their destination. They had at last arrived in the Firth of Lorne! In the distance, glinting in the evening sun, were the roofs and houses of Oban. Blackmarsh rubbed his sweaty brow. He was closing in on his clew.

3.

Whiskey & Legends

Water bridged the way into Oban as the row-boat oared to shore in the shadow of HMS Panther. Certainly, the voyage would prove to be a memorable event in the humble signalman's life, thought Jeremiah to himself. It had been his first encounter with such a glorious craft; conveyance over wave and trough had left an indelible mark on the young officer. Now, he steadied himself for the contacts that awaited him ashore. How would the locals receive him? Would it be with suspicion or with grace, he ruminated internally. The sight of a warship of the Panther's caliber, would also warrant an explanation, he started to realize. It isn't a daily ritual that the likes of a sixty-canon ship of the line pulls into to harbor, and out rows a cartographer, Blackmarsh mused to himself. Cartography! Yes! He had been in the service of the Crown, as part of his cartographic expedition. This factor could, actually, play towards the credibility of his hand, here. Were he to be so engaged, professionally, certainly, his clientele could, in like manner, include the maritime services of the navy.

With this justification in mind, Blackmarsh disembarked the row-boat and bid the Boatswain's mate adieu. It had been such a profitable encounter, that, in the time he had relied on his succor, Jeremiah Anthony had never learned his name. What a pity, he pondered. Such an upstanding and reliable youth. Verily he should be in the lad's gratitude for the aid he had rendered, without fully cognizant of the fact. The young Lieutenant touched his foot to the land and trod off the wooden craft that had delivered him to the shore of

Oban. He gave a nod of gratitude to the rowers and the mate, as they propelled back to the mother-ship, for their fated rendez-vous in Plymouth.

The village of Oban was quite small, yet the prominent features of the settlement could be easily divined by the naked eye, without need for lens or scope. A scarce array of buildings decorated the small streets of the settlement. Most prominently situated in the center was the Stevensons' Distillery. This was Jeremiah's ultimate destination. He strolled across the lane of the main street and entered the territory of the whiskey making establishment. From the outside the building struck a non-impressive chord, being of gray stone construction, with large non-descriptive longish windows embedded throughout.

Blackmarsh walked up to the arched entrance of the distillery, but was blocked by a worker, who was exiting the structure as he approached on foot.

"Caan aye render thee a servis?" said the worker.

"I'll be looking to speak with your book-keeper! My Danish client has informed me, that the wares passed to them from your factory, were not up to snuff!" said Anthony.

Blackmarsh had changed tack at the last moment, feeling the throes of inspiration upon him. He hoped that this ploy would yield the desired result. The laborer gawked at the Englishman as he spat out his complaint. Stunned for a moment, the man begged the gentleman to hold his nerve, and wait outside the eaves. Several minutes thereafter, an elder man with spectacles riding at the end of his nose, a balding pate atop his head, and rolled up white shirt-sleeves came to the door to receive the young Englishman.

"Bee ye the dulee appointèd representative of the right honorable Elias-Erik Kaspersen?" asked the clerk in awe.

"Aye. That I be. J.A. Blackmarsh. He was gravely disappointed with the quality of the stowage, and the count was off he claims. May I verify your receipts, good sir?" pronounced the Lieutenant slyly.

"Ef ye mast, but they bee all in order, I caan promise ye, Master Blackmarsh!" defended the clerk.

"Thank you, all the same. May I enter your establishment?"

"Yes, please come!" said the book-keeper, as he showed the prying signalman into his office near the door.

After ruffling through a large thoroughly combed ledger-book, the man dragged his ink-stained finger to the entry, which was less than a week old.

"See! Look fur yerself. Cargo hold filled and count verified by the skipper, Captain Amundsen. Therty-tew barrels of tha niew whiskey, and four barrels of tha matured- the eight-year brew!"

"Blast the hide off that Dane! I've been sent on a fool's errand! Please forgive the intrusion. You've been most considerate, my good man!" said Blackmarsh, wishing to eject himself from the premises.

So, he had the buyer's name, as well as the Danish captain's name. He even spotted the vessel, which was correctly rendered as "Ottar," not the "Otter" of the Dumfries paper. A minor variation, yet, Blackmarsh recorded the difference, in the case it were to yield something greater in actuality. He also had a precise date to correlate with the dates of the appearance of the abandoned vessels, should he need to.

The settlement was so puny, and the information so scant, he had begun to wonder whether, he himself, was the one who was on a "fool's errand" in this matter. Jeremiah Anthony craned his head to and fro, until he spotted the local inn and pub. Perhaps he would be able to build on his reconnaissance, by visiting the pub? Often times, with the help of the local spirits, it is possible to glean a bit of supplementary legend to a story, to which one has attached a certain gravity. It was worth a go, as he was now stranded in this wee burgh for the meanwhile. With nothing to lose, and possibly even less to gain, the stout young Lieutenant plodded over to the pub of Oban, which was graciously nestled next to the fancy-looking "Yellow House "of the settlement.

Jeremiah Anthony eyed the gathered folks in the establishment as he strolled easily up to the bar-keep. There seemed to be at least one sailor, as well as three fishermen, and a pair of rustics enjoying their drinks about the spartan pub. He ordered a large pint of the house ale and paid the stated cost without hesitation. Blackmarsh clearly stood out in this crowd, by his dress, mannerisms and speech. The dapper young Englishman sat down at the only free table, nearest the assembled sailors and fisherman, raising his drink to the locals.

"To your robust stamina, lads!" he saluted them with drink.

"Mighty kind' o ye sir!" replied one sailor with a distinct Irish accent.

The others in this man's company returned the favor to the signalman, raising mugs to his health.

"Whot bee a *Sacsannach* duin in theese parts? We gett so fuew travelers here!" said the Scottish fisherman next to the Irishman.

"Ay taught ay bee da only wone!" said the sailor, chuckling.

Blackmarsh considered his original story. Now that he was no longer on the scent of the whiskey factory, he thought, perhaps he could play to the nautical passions of the assembled men.

"As a matter of fact, I've been taken on to chart the waters around the Hebrides. The seas have proven so perilous, it seems new navigation charts are highly sought after!" explained the Lieutenant, stealthily shifting his tack.

"Well, that bee verry fine a profession, eff ye ask me!" said the older fisherman.

"Theese waters are nun tue sayfe forr the lykes of the sloppy sailor! In fact, it bee common ken round heer that a shep caan go badd, gett lost or down ryte sink below the wafe." constated the sailor.

"Oh, be that so? But how so?" inquired the curious listener.

"Heard ye not of da sheps what have turned up heer empty? No crue onbord any af dem. Most bizarr a tale is thot. Nobody is da wiser on thot score!" he cried, drawing Blackmarsh's attention to the "lost" merchant vessels.

"Ouh Angus, ett bee plane as dae! All an their bruther knows whats lurkin aut in that sea up top. In the North, aye mean." said the second fisherman, finally breaking is self-imposed code of silence.

"Pray, continue, my bonnie chum- haven't the slightest inkling what your getting at." prodded Jeremiah Anthony, now biting into his lip with pangs of curiosity, which seemed to take off like a dove in flight.

"Why, the 'Blue Men,' of course!" spat out the bronzed fisher.

"The Blue what?" a flummoxed Anthony repeated.

"The 'Blue Men of the Minch!'" he defended spitting now onto the floor in distaste. His face reddened after he had spoken, and he brought is fist down on the wooden table with his *sgian-dubh* deeply rooted into its woody flesh.

"Ethan! Awee with that naif noo! The'll bee noo faigtin in heer tonight!" yelled the simmering bar-keep.

"I've not heard tell of their likes before!" exclaimed the excited signalman. He continued his line of inquisition- "Be they foreigners to these parts?"

The assembled locals began to chuckle heartily at the Englishman's daftness. The mirth resided after several minutes of sustained laughter. Blackmarsh had begun to redden visibly in the face, at his unintended faux-pas.

"Nay! They bee the Storm Kelpies! They werk the waives an brew the sea-storms that upturn vessels. Oocasianally they steal the men off sheps, eff nout plahcahtèd by tribyutes." he said earnestly.

"That bee tru bout them Blue Men! My chum gott tayken down below once. They donned a sea-hood upon him an he saw theer great citee at the bootom of sea!" piped up the Scottish sailor.

Jeremiah Anthony Blackmarsh, was becoming annoyed by the legends of these men. He had hoped to locate a proper clew in this maze of rustics, yet, he was being sidetracked with naught but superstition and legends of yore. What of the foreigners? Surely, they had some hand in the happenings? These deeds smacked of outside intervention in British waters, as concluded by the Admiralty. Yet, at the same instant, the junior officer had no intention of insulting the beliefs of the locals, however, barmy they be.

"The Minch- what be that then?" quizzed the chubby Blackmarsh. He screwed his spectacles about on his nose, whilst he awaited a response.

"The sea off the northurn moost coost- thot bee the 'Sea of the Minch,' or simply The Minch'" explained the Scottish fisherman. He continued his cant, "naturally, moost autlanders ken naught of the playces abute heer- Scotland, thot is. Ett bee betwene the Hebrides an Scotland proper ettself."

"Aye- an a kettle of danger it contane, my sult *Sachsannach!* Ofton iz ett sed thot the Blue Men of the Minch, which we call the '*na fir ghorma,*' in the Gaelic tongue, are descendèd of the fallen angels. Sum becamm the earth fairies, sum the *na fir ghorma,* an the last becamm the northurn laites themselves!"

"Logan, duu nott call the lad 'sult'! Wher' arr yer manners?!" said Angus defensively.

"Fallen angels, I see, but I'm afraid I'm missing your point. Sult?" replied Jeremiah.

"He's callin ye fatt, mann! Etts daun raite ruud, says aye!" explained Angus.

Anthony chuckled with animation, being soon joined by the others in the tavern. It had seemed to him that his barrage of questions regarding the ships was beginning to take its toll on the hospitality and good humor of the locals. Much like the boatman, Charon, collecting a fee at the mouth of the river Styx, Blackmarsh imagined that his reputation was being claimed for a sudden death. These folk could still yield intelligence for his mission, but how to coax it from them? After some brief thought over the conundrum, the Lieutenant hatched a plan to lighten the men's tongues. Hollering over to the bar-keep, he purchased a round of whiskey for all present. Perhaps the warming of hearts could be achieved by the whetting of their palates?

A cheer of sudden exultation arose amongst the fellows gathered as they welcomed the boon of the *Sacsannach's* gift. They began singing a melody, which Blackmarsh remembered to have been a French song sung after the Battle of Malplaquet, "*Marlbrough s'en va-t-en guerre*". The words they shouted were- "For he's a jolly good fellow, for he's a jolly good fellow." It was a salute, most heartfelt to Jeremiah Anthony, and as such he basked in the momentary glory. After the chorus ceased, one of the men, his eyes swimming under the spell of the whiskey, approached the Lieutenant and tugged at his sleeve. It was the Irishman. He cupped his hand and whispered into Blackmarsh's ear.

"If ye wysh to test the veracity of the legend, hyre a boat to Ullapool, up on Loch Broom. You'll open yer eyes mann!"

The signalman nodded convincingly back, as if he valued the message, but mused to himself internally as if he had been told a cock-and-bull tale once again. The fishermen, now full of spritishness from the drink, began spinning yarns about their sea escapes as the others listened to the tall tales of the men. Meanwhile, Blackmarsh quizzed the Irishman about the ships, as the others spun their fish tales.

"Have you seen any of the ships that turned up, crew-less, I am told?" he mumbled to the Irishman.

"Aye, that oi've done, wit me yown eyes. Stripped of men on deck, they were. Even stranger, stripped of the figurehead at the head of the ships' bow! Chopped cleen aff!" exclaimed the fisher.

"That's odd, my fellow. Why impound that of all things? Surely the gear is dearer on the black trade! Were other stuffs missing from the hold?" queried Jeremiah.

"Trifles, anyways, but not tha money! Queer it was. One shep came aground aff tha north coost of Ireland at Ballycastle, the rest all en Scottish waters, according to the papers; and tha anchor was cut onn each vessel." delineated Connor, the Irish sailor.

More whiskey followed as a sailor had began to distribute wee tumblers of the amber nectar to the troupe. Connor and Jeremiah toasted with a crack of their tumblers, and downed the brew in one fell swallow. The others in the company were quick to parrot the motion, as the motion spread like an incoming wave on the shore. As the men were brimming to the apex with mirth, a balding gentleman entered the tavern. Blackmarsh turned his head to note that the entrant was none other than the book-keep from the Stevensons' Distillery.

"Come in Euan! We're jost havin a bit of the pryde of Oban, with this luvly fella!"

"A spot af the Oban *'uisge'* as we say up here! So how fares tha Dane's bloody emissary?" he said contemptuously.

"Whot say ye, Euan, whot emissary? This man bee a cartographer en truth!" explained Angus insistently.

 Blackmarsh began to redden as a sea of eyes turned on him. A sense of unease began to burgeon in his belly.

"Aye, say this fella is a Dane spy, sent overe heer to steele the Stevensons' whiskey recipe! Came into the factory, nosing aboot. Claimed to bee an emissary for a foreign client, only, aye look'd ett upp, didn't aye, an thot client has another man altogether!" accused the book-keep.

"He tauld uss he bee mappin the coost! Repulsive liar! We've a spy- thot bee shur!" howled the bar-keep from his post.

"This is a general misunderstanding, my good people!" said Jeremiah Anthony in haste. The gang seized him with their muscly arms and dragging him into the street, beginning a tug of war with the surprised, and now wholly alarmed *Sacsannach*. Lifting his feet from the ground the troupe heaved him atop their heads and moved across the road, to the edge of firth. At this vantage a sheer drop, of a man's height, gaped upwards. The gleeful mariners began to sing a local tune as they heaved Blackmarsh into the swell. The

Lieutenant, flummoxed at the sudden loss of his cover, hit the water like a sack of Ulster potatoes, causing a dramatic back-splash. The men walked back into the tavern laughing raucously. J.A. Blackmarsh had been unceremoniously launched into the firth- stern to aft!

4.

The Clew of the Minch

Jeremiah Anthony Blackmarsh had fallen short of his own goal. In vacillating his alias he had exposed himself to revelation by the local dwellers. This lesson had to be learned, if he was to expunge his error to skirt jeopardy in the future. Unlike a dog which returns to its vomit, Blackmarsh pledged to heed the value attained in this bitter defeat, and avoid its reproduction. After his fall from glory, the Lieutenant trod back to the settlement and took lodgings at the inn. He would need to strip out of his wet tog, pantaloons and leggings, dry his bluchers and warm himself with a splash of brandy or whiskey. His bet was that the establishment certainly stocked the Obanite amber. As a result of his plunge, Blackmarsh had lost his spectacles. This represented a half loss to him, as he could see in the distance without their aid, however, reading up close would prove a challenge for the portly Lieutenant.

Seeking to look over his soggy map of the Scotch coast, Anthony removed the article from his waterlogged bodice. The signalman spread out the long map across a table in his chamber to dry. He perused its wet surface and hovered his finger above it until he came to the small fishing town of Ullapool. This unfamiliar locale would be his ultimate destination, as it hugged the Minch, nestled quietly in Loch Broom. Blackmarsh pondered over the best approach. One possibility would be to go north, above Oban, deep into the Highlands, through the locks up through the old trails and forts of the Jacobite Uprising of 1745. This route would take him through the ruins of Fort William at the foot of Ben Nevis, across Loch Ness, through Fort August, and eventually terminate at Inverness. From there he would still require a vessel to sail around the extreme north of Scotland, back to the westward portion of the coast where Ullapool was. Certainly this was a longer route. The other route would be wholly nautical, taking him, by boat, into the narrow channel between the mainland and Mull Isle. Thus, up this skinny neck of water known as the Sound of Mull; onward following the coast of the mainland; from hence traversing Loch Ash, between Skye Island and the western coast, and eventually up into the Minch and towards Ullapool.

Time was beginning to weigh heavily on Jeremiah Anthony; within days it would be August. If he could hire a craft, captained by a reliable pilot, he could hope to make the most hasty progress to his destination at Ullapool. It would also bring him into the Minch, which was the area where he gathered the ships had suffered their presumed attack by forces, as yet unknown. For now, Anthony could dine and mull over both options mentally, considering the merits and pitfalls of each. By morning he must, by all rigors, come to a final conclusion as to his ploy in the matter; if, of course, he was not influenced by other external factors in the meanwhile. Blackmarsh headed down for his dinner.

***

Captain Evans sat at the end of the table, fiddling with a tankard of ale. His neighbor, a fellow mariner from his own vessel, a merchant ship bearing the name of "Sea-Dragon," was engrossed in his pewter plate of food, which was handsomely prepared with shavings of beef and gravy on toasted bread rolls. Mrs. MacNiven, the owner of the inn, seemed to have a firm grip on the belly of her guests. She knew how to feed them, and would be sure to welcome many back, as a result of her highly satisfactory culinary arts. Jeremiah Anthony, having for the most part dried out, also dined on the chipped beef and gravy over toasted bread rolls, and was devoting his attention to an after-diner dram of the "blood of Oban." Certainly the Stevenson brothers could be content that their malt whiskey was the drink of choice for the local merchants, as well as their guests.

The fact that there were merchant vessels harbored in the port did not escape Lt. Blackmarsh's notice. On top of this, the sliver of chance that had materialized nearly in his own lap, with a sea captain at table and under the same roof of the inn was to Jeremiah, less than a guaranteed outcome, but certainly more than blind luck. He had drifted into a comfy middle terrain betwixt the two, which had brought him into the vicinity of an individual who could bring him closer to unraveling the clew of the Minch. But what could tempt the Captain and his mate to lend a sympathetic ear to his pressing errand? For starters he must cut a crisp impression on the fellow, demonstrating the solidity of his character, seriousness of purpose, and finally, his solvency of pocket. The last of these factors Anthony deemed as the easiest to make in evidence; the others required a succinct rendition of charisma. and the tender application of persuasion. To pull it off, he must, needs, muster his talents of social charm, while driving towards his intended shore. He had after all achieved this recently, with regards to the Duke of Wellington, and his supreme confidence in electing him to this mission. Surely he could do it once more, in mastering the likes of the oceanic skipper?

Blackmarsh cursorily made an ocular examination of the man. The Captain was one of those chums with a rugged bark-like skin. Lashed by sun and waves, he had obviously seen much in his maritime profession. A prominent scar was visible on the man's right cheek-bone, which he occasionally caressed with his right thumb. The Lieutenant ventured forward in engaging the man in conversation.

"You strike me as a man worth his salt, Captain Evans."

"Why say you that, Mr...pardon what are you called?" replied the old sea-dog.

"Blackmarsh. Jeremiah Blackmarsh. It's simply, even in my small years, a man has to be a fool not to clap eyes on an Odysseus. That scar- you wear it as a badge of honor. That suggests to me a man one can count on in the execution of matters of importance. I should not like to see the bloke or beast behind that story concerning the scar's origin!"

Evans let out a roar of laughter at the young Lieutenant.

"Well said lad! Your import is received; but of what seek you? A vessel, a captain, or both?" said the Captain point-blank and frank.

"I'm over a barrel. My employer has tasked me with charting the coast. I require passage to Ullapool, and no awkward questions. Can it be done, and at what cost?" replied Blackmarsh in jargon he reckoned the Captain would grasp.

"Any job can be done, any route charted; the key to this lock is what kind of coin can be mustered for the job? You look like a fella with deep-pockets. I like that. I also like coin in hand at the outset." said the elder man, stroking the scar with two fingers. now

The mate had all but ceased his mastication and was engaged with spilling ale on his shirt, as he slurped noisily from the tankard. The signalman stuck his thumb into the partially dried bodice and wormed a golden Half-guinea out. This he settled on the table in view of the Captain.

"I figured one of these upfront, a twin to follow when we reach target. Would that be fair enough, under the captain's dispatch log?" queried the signalman in a buoyant humor.

"It's a bargain Blackmarsh. We were headed yonder all the same. A tad further wont upset my crew."

"One last stipulation, my work is pressing. May we depart on the morrow? Time is waning to waste and naught." explained the young officer.

"I figure we ought to pull anchor at six of the clock, then. Does that fit with you, boy?"

"I'll have Mrs. MacNiven rouse me at five. Thank you, Evans. A pleasure transacting the affair under your auspices, I can assure you." stated the Lieutenant.

"The same." fired back the laconic sea-dog.

Jeremiah withdrew the golden coin and slipped it back into his bodice. The Captain's eyes followed both the coin and hand of the young man until he felt the eyes of the lad upon his countenance.

"When we've lifted anchor, my good sir." said the signalman, as he nodded for the evening and returned back to his chamber.

"Good night then, young Blackmarsh. See you on the morrow at harbor! Do not tarry to the appointment!" bleated Evans to Jeremiah's turned back.

The young Lieutenant signaled waving his hand in the air, without turning to his senior interlocutor.

***

The simultaneous crowing of a cock, and Mrs. MacNevin's banging at Jeremiah's door, went off like a double instance of thunder, clapping at his periphery. He roused himself and, after paying the last of his bill, gathered his bag, dried clothes and all, and set off for the harbor. Once there, he sat on a stone wall and watched the mates onboard the Sea-Dragon working on the ship's rigging and preparing other equipment for the chartered voyage to Ullapool. Stocks were still being loaded and shifted in the hold. The ship itself was a two masted brig with a white painted trim, spanning the port holes along the length of the ship.

Jeremiah fixed his telescope to the ship's outline, scanning the vessel from forecastle to the aft quarterdeck. The brig looked every ounce a swift craft, having no cannon onboard, and evidently less than half full with ballast. His fastidiousness for a hasty voyage was within reach, he reasoned.

Fishing his breakfast provisions out of his sack- the items he had paid for while departing the inn- he found wrapped in dark paper, a wedge of hard Scottish cheese, four bread-rolls, and a large bottle of ale. Onion greens where also neatly tucked into the side of the provision, independently wrapped in a rolled up bit of gazetteer paper. With the last moments on dry-land, Lt. Blackmarsh munched the spartan rations with a sense of impending adventure. He would soon be cutting the waves of the Minch onboard the Sea-Dragon. The scent of discovery was ripe in his nostrils, followed by the taste of progress in his entrusted duty, he imagined, as he masticated onion greens and bread, with occasional swigs of ale.

Approaching six o'clock, he saw that Captain Evans had come topside, and was strutting about the quarterdeck, apparently busy giving orders to the crew. Jeremiah stood up and went over to the peer. He watched as a transfer boat rowed up to his position and flagged him over to jump in. After the passenger was seated, the rower turned to navigate back to the Sea-Dragon and Blackmarsh was allowed to scale netting, which jutted over the side, granting him ingress to the main deck and a subtle welcome by the 1st Mate, once his feet were planted aboard.

Blackmarsh, having come to a decision as to the route, had wagered it best to hug the coastline for as long as possible. He explained his proposed rout to Evans, who nodded silently at the routing. Captain Evans, having determined that everything was in order for an early departure, gave the order for the anchor to be raised. The Sea-Dragon had begun its lurch towards the Sea of the Minch and Ullapool.

***

A harsh wind buffeted the Sea-Dragon as it headed north-northeasterly. A rhythmic lapping of the waves against the hull created the perfect semblance of motion, which pacified Jeremiah's urgency in obtaining the distant shore he'd been whispered about in the tavern at Oban. What exactly could he expect there? Would it be in line with the tales of the Blue Men? Or would he find another clew out of the maze of the mystery of the lost crews and abandoned ghost vessels? This bit of intelligence he'd garnered from the Irish sailor had simmered in his brain like a kettle of half-cooked fish. He was relying on the sea-dog to throw him a good bone. This bone, he hoped, would be attached to sinews, that would bring him into contact with the mysterious perpetrators of the attacks on merchant shipping.

As the Lieutenant looked out to sea, he could see the distant shores of Eigg and Rhum islands, which instead of passing through the straits nearer the mainland, the Sea-Dragon's course was deeper to sea- plowing a channel towards the Little Minch. Jeremiah Anthony withdrew his telescope and examined the visual references he had learned from the map. It was true, they were headed into deeper waters, away from his proscribed course. Why were they off course? The portly signalman hobbled on the rocking vessel back to the quarterdeck where Evans was standing near the helmsman.

"Evans, I see we're skirting the mainland. Is this intentionally?" queried Blackmarsh.

"Those waters are too treacherous to traverse. We're moving into the open channel for the best wind-speed on top of that." replied the Captain.

"Can't argue with that, Captain. Very sound navigation." exclaimed Jeremiah Anthony.

"Young Blackmarsh, there's the matter of coin, that's grown overdue. We agreed a Guinea in gold, did we not?" said Evans.

"Yes. Half up front and half at landfall." agreed the signalman.

"I reckon we should alter that agreement. What about you? Let's say, I'll have all your gold. That's what I'll be wanting!" blurted the Captain.

"What kind of picaroon breaks his word!" shrieked the surprised Lieutenant.

"Tie 'em up and throw 'em into the 1st Mate's quarters!" spat out the scar-faced buccaneer.

The Mate had already drawn his pistol and coaxed Blackmarsh into the room under the quarterdeck. Once liberated of his money and firmly tied, Lt. Jeremiah Anthony Blackmarsh found himself a prisoner, on board the pirate ship Sea-Dragon.

5.

Seaward Bound

Time is a luxury, which not all of us are blessed with. In the case of Jeremiah Anthony Blackmarsh, he had blundered into a piratical syndicate of loathsome types. Certainly his time was up, in the matter of the lost crews and abandoned ships. He had up to this point failed in the service of his commander, Wellington. Now he was swept away with a sea-wash of acrid defeat and salty imprisonment. What other injury would he suffer, and the accompanying indignities, that were tethered with, as if chained? The rope bindings on his wrists and ankles, left little wiggle-room for escape. In like manner, he had been gagged with a kerchief over the mouth, and blinded by a hood covering his eyes. In the adjacent chamber, he could hear some of the men rolling dice for his effects. His map, telescope, and even the razor he had secreted, had been discovered and purloined. Feeling much as a flightless bird of the northern icy sea, Blackmarsh was going to have to reason through his escape, if he were to have a remote chance of survival at the hands of such privateers. But how?

The likes of such riffraff as the crew of the Sea-Dragon were the sort that could smell profit miles away. Evans had sized up the green signalman fairly accurately, suspecting that he had deep-pockets and little experience in the ways of the sea-faring world. The prospect of such a combination of favorable factors entering his sphere of control had proved too cumbersome to resist, and too tempting a prize to allow egress from his demesne. It was simply a matter of choosing the proper time and locale to pounce on the cornered prey. In the case of Blackmarsh, the time had presented itself sooner than expected, as opposed to the later, which would have, doubtless, been in due time at any rate.

Where were they sailing to? And for what purpose? These were the pair of principle points of interest, which now teased Jeremiah's brain. If he could comprehend their moves, and motives, perhaps this could open up a window of opportunity for escape? This was the angle of attack that the Lieutenant now fixed his cerebral rumination to solve.

In the matter of motivation, Anthony considered his subject matter with a generalized approach- this be money, gold, and valuable commodities to trade in. This lot were the true profit-seekers, out to evade the trap of the working bloke, roving the sea in search of a treasure haul of some magnitude to chase away the ghost of poverty. As they had been in Oban, and had taken on cargo, it was likely to suppose that the highest value commodity they had acquired was that of the whiskey barrels, that the corsairs had taken onboard. If the whiskey were a legitimate trade for the buccaneers, then they would be running this at a substantial profit, he imagined. If the trade were to be illicit, they would likely be in league with someone at the Stevensons' distillery, with extra barrels in tow, which had likely been written off as spoilage or ruined during the manufacture of the stuff. It was sensible to suppose that Euan was their wolf in the fold, having a cut of the profits. Only the book-keeper stood in a position to release the merchandise, fub the barrel count of the manifest, and likewise, the shipping logs to account for each haul.

Jeremiah's reasoning indicated that the price of legitimate trade would render the cargo too costly to be had by most buyers. As this ballast was unlawful, Evans was likely hard-pressed to flog the stuff at a lower rate to speed up its vanishing from his cargo-hold. In this way, he could offer it to sleepy ports and towns around the Scottish or Irish coast as fast as he could manage. This, therefore, was his most like modus operandi. Blackmarsh's own unfortunate presence had merely offered an easy course to plot for ancillary coin prospecting. In addition to this, he would also have been a true god-send to the marauders, since, as he was quite unknown to the locals, he would also tend to be easily forgotten, and particularly not missed by anyone, with whom they had regular contact. Aye, it was a shortfall from grace, he reckoned he had suffered at their hands. Jeremiah had gone from being at the apex, straight to the bilge!

Escaping could likely only be managed at feeding time; that is unless Jeremiah Anthony were not to be asked to "walk the plank." Still, what profit would this bring them? If this syndicate was deep in the black waters of whiskey running, they may also have truck with slavers. Many of those who do trade with Caribbean traders deal in human bondage. The corsairs and pirates off Tripoli, and the other Barbary pirates, were a prime example of such ransom-seeking riffraff. Many of these bandit fiefdoms in Africa, too, easily did business with anyone with an eye to paying for the commodity of their own or neighboring peoples; such was the painful destiny of many a Blackamoor sent off to the colonies, and to the other destinations in the New World.

The secondary obstacle facing the Lieutenant was chiefly that, on the off-chance he managed to escape his binds, there was also the matter of his being stranded on the Sea-Dragon in the midst of the sea. How could he overcome the additional obstacle? Once freed, Blackmarsh would be surrounded by the foes who had captured him, thus all of his efforts would clearly be for naught. This eventuality led him to consider a mental ruse of some devising. If he could persuade or hatch a plausible mind trick on the gang, he would stand the most optimum possibility of success. This ploy, consisting less in brawn, and more in brain, would have the greatest yield, if he considered its proper substance, employment and timing. He would mull this over until he had reached the surest hypothesis.

***

Two days had come and gone while Jeremiah Anthony became used to the routines of the pirates. He had been allowed freedom of movement only twice each day to eat, and he was let up on deck to answer nature's call immediately afterwards. These times coincided with his breakfast, in the morning, and before bedding, at night. The signalman reckoned that, should he be able to manage his bolt at the night loosening, he could attempt his escape at that hour alone. Once free and on deck, he could grab a glowing lantern, climb the rigging of the sails, and threaten to put the cloth of the sails to the flame. Should he burn the sails, the ship would merely flounder dangerously in the water, and become mired in the sea, as a buoy, dead in the water, to drift as the ocean saw fit.

Once he had the attention of the Captain, he could demand a row-boat and provisions, to be lowered for his escape. As he saw the matter, this would be his singular option to alight. Once in the boat, he could drift away into the darkness and out of their grasp. The entire escape would be a gambit, but what other alternative did the young Lieutenant have? To be sold off as chattels in slavery would be an ignoble end for him, which he wished to avoid at any cost. The other option Anthony considered was that he may be killed or maimed by the wild buccaneers, should his worth to them diminish. Every other mental trick of his concoction would rely on his persuasion and their gullibility. With the fright of burning the sails, he considered this to be the heaviest trump card he held in the hand of his pure bluff. To this ploy Jeremiah would adhere, awaiting the gentle fall of night.

Time seemed to drag on at a tedious and leisurely stroll. As Blackmarsh waited, he pictured his escape execution over and over in his brain. The sea swelled and rocked the vessel as the hours lurched by. This pattern only seemed to increase as time ticked to the vanguard ahead. The scullion came down earlier than usual to remove the hood and gag. As he did so, he announced that the sea was in revolt, and a storm was brewing "swifter than a falcon with an appetite." The captive was in this light, therefore, to be fed inside and not allowed out to answer to his privy needs. This development would all, but, flatten his planned escape. The young officer had to think of something to save his plan, or pounce to the change and adapt a new strategy. As he ate, Anthony, began to re-organize his plan. What he needed was calm weather. The storm, which was brewing up, had interrupted his concoction, arresting it prematurely. This began to infuriate him. At each step he had been getting the short straw of the bunch! His dander was now bubbling up in high dudgeon. He felt a violence building to force, like a tropical gale within him.

As he finished the bowl of gruel he had been handed, the scullion approached him for the bowl. In the split of an eye, he wielded it in an upward arc and landed it into the jawbone of the scullion, who hit the deck flat. Using the bit of ropes that had been used for his own hands, Jeremiah deftly roped the hands of the scullion, then undid the knotted rope of his own feet. These were tied in a double diamond knot, which made for undoing the thing quite an affair. Luckily the scullion was out cold. By the looks of his face, Blackmarsh had broken his jaw. Slipping out of the last of his bonds, he tied up the scullion, set the jawbone as best he could manage, so that a great rope ball kept the mouth sealed from speaking, although there was little danger of this prospect, currently. Anthony slipped the red headscarf on his head and took the blue sash around his waist as well, to cloak himself from a distance from instant recognition and betrayal. Perchance this emulation and obfuscation could purchase a needed delay, he wondered?

Up on deck, he could see the night sky had descended and with the rock of the crashing waves. All hands were battening down the hatches and retracting the sails. As soon as he appeared, the junior signalman heard orders barked at him to see to the flapping sails. Playing his role, Jeremiah quickly rushed to the starboard side. He mimicked the motion of the other buccaneers, in the pandemonium. The white spew of the waves was as a curtain about the men, as they fought the wind, the water, and the rolling of the vessel, to and fro.

At the place where J.A. had found himself, he spied a row-boat, which was being buffeted from the side of the ship violently. Gazing across the vicinity, he looked for anything of remote use. Wedged into some netting on the adjacent mast, he could see a long knife jutting out by the hand-shaped pommel. It resembled a Saracen's blade, or a rather miniature scimitar. He decided to take this, while that side of the ship was clean of pirates. All hands were busy with subduing the elements. He grabbed it and eyed the row-boat.

It was too tempting not to resist, even in the face of the tumult of the sea. Blackmarsh rushed up to the boat and began to unfasten it. The ropes of the craft were tangled someplace farther up its line. It seemed no use, as they were quite adeptly moored down for the storm. Jeremiah withdrew the knife and hastily began slicing through the thick fibrous cord of the moorings. He had rooted out the weak link of the rope, where he was able to free it totally, causing the small craft to lurch down into the swelling sea.

"Hey you! What are ye doing there ye daft fool?!" shrieked the 1st Mate.

Blackmarsh wasted no time. He dove over into the sea and grabbed the rope which dangled outside the rowboat. After one swell, he was literally heaved into the precarious craft and hunkered himself in the bottom under the plank-board seats. As the storm intensified he lost sight of the Sea-Dragon, which was receiving blows from the sea at an alarming rate of fire. Being so weighted down with the cargo of the whiskey, seemed to work against it, in light of the storm. The sound of splintering masts could be discerned between wave crashes, as the brigantine crept into the doomy darkness of the night storm.

***

Jeremiah awoke under an over cropping of land. It was evidently a very narrow sea-cave. The sandy, rocky floor was littered with occasional sea shells, and was slightly open to the sky and sea at its mouth. It was quite fortunate that the time within its recess had been spent, it seemed, was in a period of low-tide, as by the look of the walls, the place tended to flood upwards at high-tide. The water-mark on the limestone was evident, even in the dimness of the shallow hallow. The sense of a throbbing ache came from the top of his head. He had likely struck his head during the violent tossing of the row-boat during the storm. His escape-craft had, either broken up, or drifted away in the swirl of water; whereas he had been ejected and, he being rather buoyant, glided into the safety of the cave. A distant memory of childhood came rushing into his mind like a sea spray. This place, where he now found himself, would have been called a "fat-man's squeeze" by his chums of youth.

Where was he? The place was an island in the Hebrides, to his mind, judging by the amount of time the Sea-Dragon had been sailing. Had they turned southward, it could be a small island off Ireland, he reasoned. Anthony exited the sea-cave slowly and peered into the sky, and then back to land. He was on the edge of an island that seemed enormously long, and barren. The Lieutenant peered in the other direction where he saw what appeared to be a cluster of trees near the shore. Recalling the layout of the geography he had reckoned that this could possibly be Lewis Island. If so, it was the largest island in the Hebrides. He judged by the position of the sun, over the ridge of the island that he was on the western coast, and the sea to his back was thus the North Atlantic.

If his observations were correct, it meant likely the craft had sailed towards Ullapool, traversed the Sea of the Minch, and turned to round the island's northern most tip. So the storm that hit occurred at the terminus of the Sea of the Minch. Just like the legends of the fishermen had claimed! How oddly reality had mirrored their tales. Yet, it was often the case that tales were grounded in some basic aspect of reality. The point of departure from that reality came of its own wild accord, and spawned a legend of its own.

The Lieutenant's ruminations ceased for the moment. He decided to plod on over to look about and see about securing aid or rescue from his predicament. After ambling a dozen paces, he was seized by the vision of a vessel at sea. It's anchor had been deployed and it was grounded off coast, abreast the shoreline. Squinting to see the form, Blackmarsh could just make out its outline. It was the Sea-Dragon! The masts had been terribly shattered by the winds and water; the sails were hanging down in tatters about the vessel. A small launch had set out from the island with a solitary figure rowing out to the stranded ship. They had clearly signaled for aid, but their sorry state could nearly be deduced by a blind-man.

Jeremiah Anthony Blackmarsh was fortunate to have his life, but everything else he had provisioned was gone. Even the Saracen blade he had used to free the boat while escaping was lost to the fury of the sea. He mustn't tussle again with that crew, if he could skirt its materialization! This would end in his recapture, surely. Even in their current state, the buccaneers could surround and recapture him, he considered carefully. For the moment he opted to wait and watch what came to pass with the pirates, and wither they would depart. Certainly, the man coming to their rescue would be doomed, he judged by their villainous nature.

As the launch pulled up, he could see a barrel get towed up, with a crate soon to follow. The fellows were being given succor, brought from the man's camp, it appeared, in the theater before him. In the distance, the signalman could even hear singing and could discern that the bunch were drinking and eating. If they were as famished as he currently felt, then they would be capable of digesting a full course meal, and whetting their palates with lovely rum or ale. Blackmarsh's own empty gullet rebelled at his hunger, which felt to him as a tantalized void, while witnessing the feast. The storm must have ruined their supplies, or in the tumult of the wild waves, been jettisoned overboard. The pirates' financial losses would be ruinous, he speculated, causing even more sacking and plunder on their part.

Within the hour all the merriment had died down and, little movement was visible from the ship. The rescuer, a burly creature, was unloading some materiel from the ship, which he lowered back down into his launch. After he managed this, he returned alone and rowed back to shore with his haul. As nothing stirred from the wrecked quarterdeck of the Sea-Dragon, Blackmarsh wondered what precisely had occurred? If only he had had his nautical telescope at hand to better espy the happenings there. The burly giant continued unloading his cargo and proceeded back to the ship, repeating the process once again.

It was all very odd to the signalman, and he began to smell rottenness in this business. Were the two parties business associates of the same syndicate? Were they smuggling something valuable to the island? So many questions and, yet so difficult to obtain any firm answers at this vantage. If Jeremiah ventured forth to spy on the man's encampment, he would surely be seen. It was not certain, what kind of figure this was, and whether he could be relied on for assistance. The odds were in favor of him being in league with the brigands, which, if his idea held its water, would blacken him as an enemy, dangerous to the Lieutenant's own person.

The man disappeared into the wood-grove with the cargo he had pulled in and began to work therein. The curiosity of the matter gnawed at Blackmarsh. He must seek a better vantage point to observe their dealings and see for himself! He wondered whether it would be better to effect his espionage under the cloak of darkness at nightfall? This would reduce the chance of him being seen, at any rate. Yes. This had got to be the answer. For the meanwhile, Anthony decided to return to the sea-cave and attempt to locate something edible. Perhaps he could dig up cockles or mussels to tame his ravishing hunger pangs?

Jeremiah Anthony Blackmarsh returned stealthily back to his "fat-man's squeeze" and began upturning the sandy beach, finding a handful of mollusks to consume. As he farmed these from the edge of the seabed, he remembered an old tune about Molly Malone- the Irish fishmonger who carted cockles and mussels about Dublin. It contented him to remember the tune, as he farmed his rations out from the sea's perimeter.

The hours dragged until night began to fall. With this came the rising of the water in the cave. High tide was beginning to return in a swift stride! Jeremiah fled the cave and resumed his old spot, from whence he had spied on the islander during the morning. The sky was a dim black, and the sun had all but faded from the western horizon when Blackmarsh scurried closer to the wood-grove. A blaze erupted in the center of a clearing within this miniature wood-thicket. Jeremiah beheld it as such a wonder as he crept up to the woods. This feature was quite a rare oddity, as he had always understood the features of the Hebrides to be a bare and harsh land, nestled on the craggy rocks and green grasses near the great Atlantic.

The light shining out of the place was a great torch burning brightly, much like a beacon. It was then, that the figure of men could be seen up in the trees. The forms were familiar to the Lieutenant. It was the remnants of the crew from Sea-Dragon. They were tied and roped, hanging down from the limbs of the trees, one of which was a great oak. They were ensnared! Several dead men were also lifelessly hanging from above, with throats cut. Blood had trickled down from the horrible wounds.

A burly naked man stood underneath the buccaneers, with a curved knife in hand. The man's skin seemed quite dark in the flickering of the flame. As he peered to view the figure, Blackmarsh was battered down by what he saw. This huge man- he was wholly painted in a deep indigo blue!

6.

Sacred Duty

Fearful now, the figure before the signalman flashed his blade in the torchlight. As he cut the flesh, an eerie chant fell from his malevolently quivering lips. Ichor ignominious and crimson, flowed from the veins of the anchored captives. Before these lost men, the blue figure of the man took up the red flow with a sacrificial bowl, which he offered up reverently to the great oak. His victims hung vicariously suspended by damnably thick hempen cords. The sight of the sacrifice was macabre; sinister without hesitation of mind. Jeremiah Anthony maintained his distance and remained hidden. He dared not to expose himself to attack. The bump on his head was still tender, and his body still ached from his wreckage on the beach. In addition to this, he was as yet, still unarmed. His opponent, on the contrary was a huge towering man, and quite sufficiently armed; both factors galling and additive of the Lieutenant's chagrin.

Blackmarsh pivoted his head to the rear to view the faded light from behind him. This was a flickering illumination emanating from inside a large cave. This creature must inhabit that place, he reckoned to himself. Perhaps, whilst he was occupied with the slaughter, the signalman could examine the place for a weapon to overpower the lanky, muscled fellow? It was worth a gamble.

The stealthy Lieutenant lurked amongst the shadows behind the grove, and approached the cave cautiously. The only stirring therein issued from a thick candle, contained within a lantern, which burned faintly, yet allowed sufficient light to view some of the cave's contents. There were large stores of crates stacked at the far end, and many hanging contraptions with glass bottles. These were filled with seeds, kernels, grasses, and leaves. Furs lined a make-shift pile of stones, which evidently served as a crude bed for the man. The conditions were quite rudimentary- wild even.

Below the clay lamp, was a stone altar topped with many carved stone idols and other figures of bone, teeth and tusks. A thick leather-bound manual lay open atop the altar. Upon the book rested a goose-feather quill and a jar of ink of oak galls. The writing of this tome was in English, however, it reflected a distinct style and rhythm. This to Blackmarsh's mind resembled devotional poetry! He read from several lines on the open right-hand page:

When mannish imps crush under foot the sacred sprig-

Flay the offender swiftly, revive the revered twig!

Summon the slumbering Selkie!

Fetch hither the timeless Kelpie!

Under the wrath of the wicked ones, those vile prigs-

Who deign to fell trees, sacred and big!

Let them sprightly inherit the welkin!

A ceremony of Druids in the spellken!

These ruinous and godless lines shrieked from the parchment at Jeremiah like a raving banshee. He was utterly flummoxed at their appearance. The more of the poetry he parsed, the greater his revulsion grew. Like a satyr serenading him with a sickening melody, he had begun to feel waves of panic surround him. Pandemonium filled his soul, as if he was stranded on an island of savages, intent only on a blind desire for blood-lust and the gore of impious ritual. Seized by the clutches of this dread, the young officer sped from the cavern, returning in the direction of the fat-man's squeeze.

He arrived at the cave unnoticed, and as yet, unharmed. This fortune was short-lived, as the cave was, to him, inaccessible due to the high evening tide. The Lieutenant had got to find a fresh hideout to secret himself from the bloody tree-priest, before he became the next line of poetry in the man's profane book.

Searching the coast, Blackmarsh could spot nothing suitably big enough for his girth. He began to scour the island for something relevant for his refuge. After some effort, and limited by the rays of a cold and distant half-moon, he was able to locate a thicket of bushes, which he could hide himself comfortably inside. There was even a small crevice, into which he could partially hide, amongst the high grasses around him.

A direct view of the druid's campsite and grove were visible from his nest, without being close enough to be spotted. The Lieutenant settled into his natural dugout and wondered- was this wretched figure the cause of the disappearance of those crews? Could it be he had stumbled onto the source of his quest? Tethered to this supposition, he recollected the legend he heard of the local folk; it was of the legend of the Blue Men of the Minch he paused to consider. Was this druid of their ilk? He had certainly been of normal color by daylight, the fleshy hue of a Scotsman, he had figured. Now by night this very same creature had assumed the blueness of the old Celtic warriors. Surely this was due to a ritual washing with woad, he posed in thought? Blackmarsh, always interested in the history of yore, had read much of the stories of the Celtic tribes. These, too, in their time, had effected an indigo blue war painting for battle. This evoked a fierce semblance towards their foes during battle.

The theory was plausible. This wayward recluse had adopted the old ways, and become a protector of the plant. Secluded from society on this lone and faraway shore, he followed the wisdom of the ancients of his people, and had become a killer of men, in the service of his sacred office. From the silence of his cave, with only the crash of the sea in hearshot, he scribed druidic poetry and prayers to the holy objects of his devotion. Yet, this was all an incredible revelation to the signalman. How could this fierce, wild man of the Outer Hebrides overwhelm crews of sailors in his singularity of purpose alone? He must have aid or succor; allies to his cause; co-followers, or others in league with him in this banal worship. Jeremiah Anthony, his hunger still deeply welling in the hollow of his gullet, drifted into a guarded night slumber as the peril of his thought eclipsed him. He had succumbed to the shock of discovery.

****

On the following morning, Lt. Blackmarsh awoke to the sweet island melody of bird-song. From the wood-grove, birds had settled into the leaves and branches of the trees, making music with serene calls to their nestled ilk. The fact that this outcast had planted and nurtured such a singularly resplendent glade in the hostile barrens of the island, was a feat naturally laudable of significant merit. This was unarguably a noble endeavor. However, his human sacrifices to the wood and sea spirits indicated an intellect that had sailed into a marshy coastline at low-tide. Stranded in such a morass, he had marked himself as an opponent to both the common-folk of the realm, as much as to the authorities. Even should this wayward druid prove not to be the cause of the consternation over the mysteriously vanishing crews, Jeremiah's duty was clear. He would have to neutralize this unsavory injurious mudlark by hook or by crook. This presented a problem for Anthony. He was essentially stranded on a foreign shore, no-less weaponless, and lamentably alone. How could he hope to rid the isles of that star-gazing, shrub-worshiping menace?

Blackmarsh considered his options and current limitations. He was nearly starving, had no practical arms about his person, was at the disadvantage of not being able to spy his opponent's actions, being unaided by his trusty telescope, and was a mere force of one. Yet, was he alone? If he was verily on Lewis Island, he was on the largest island in the Outer Hebrides. Certainly farther up the coast, on the other side of the island, there would be settlements and folk residing there. This, however, would be another challenge. He would have to cover miles and miles, over barren terrain to get to the other side of the island, and his presence on the upper reaches, near the apex of the island's ridge, would absolutely summon the gaze of the druid. In his exhausted state, he would not fare well in outpacing the fellow. If caught, it would be *he*, suspended from the great oak at the center of the secluded grove!

The hour was presently small, being yet morning. This would equate in a present low-tide at the fat-man's squeeze. Perhaps he could crawl back to the cave and settle in for a summary breakfast of freshly-dug cockles and muscles from its cloistered beach at the mouth? Food-foraging was definitely his most pressing requirement at hand. Priority for survival would only benefit his overall goal, yet, at the same time, he worried about the erosion of time for his mission. The precious days were slipping by, once more, and he must, too, formulate a strategy to overcome the druid, in order to accomplish his charge of the Admiralty. With these priorities fixed lucidly in his mind, Jeremiah Anthony began to inch slowly, at a snail's pace, back in the direction of his old fat-man's squeeze.

Moving as he was, below eye-level, afforded him stealth, but at the cost of his own surveillance of the druid's base. Occasionally, the signalman would cautiously raise his head up, slowly, like a tortoise extending his neck to peer about. Each time he had done this, he was not able to observe any motion at the base below. The tree-man was, no doubt, in the cave resting for his nocturnal nefariousness; or, possibly even penning his poetic forest praises. Whatever the cause of this silence, Blackmarsh made his slow progress back to the sea-cave without hindrance. A few times on the way, seagulls had circled him, betraying his position with their boisterous caws of alarm. Happily, these alarms had gone unobserved or unrecorded by the opponent below.

At last, back at the fat-man's squeeze, Blackmarsh begun his sea-harvest, and busily gobbled the sea-fresh sustenance from its sunken locale. This raw food was not to his usual liking, but in light of his predicament, he was content to receive nourishment of some kind. The young officer's palate watered for an unobtainable pint of ale, or a bonnie tumbler of the "blood of Oban," which he had sampled at the wee settlement on the Firth of Lorne. All in good time, he assured himself optimistically.

After his cold breakfast, Jeremiah laid against the firm cave-
bed and thought to himself. He was intent on facing this
villain, but how? Should he opt for a physical attempt or,
rather, another mental ploy to handle this menace? In this
environment, the Lieutenant could likely locate a sharp,
jagged stone to use as a pointed weapon. His opponent, on
the other hand, was a giant of a man. His height had to span
well over six feet. He was also built like a Scythian of old.
Jeremiah, by contrast, was of average height, portly, and
weakened by both undernourishment and the elements. The
contest would be as imbalanced as could be expected.
Blackmarsh would be at a grand disadvantage, on the merits
of brawn alone.

His own chances for success lay abundantly in favor of
applying his intellect to win against the druid. To do this, he
must understand the fellow's weaknesses. Currently, as
Jeremiah Anthony ruminated on the nature of his enemy, he
was possessed of a dearth of any evident weaknesses in any
abundance. Everything he pondered seemed to reveal his
opponent's surfeit of advantages. He was well-fed, and well-
rested; robust in strength and girth; had an intimate
knowledge of the surroundings; and most keenly, armed and
fanatical in his purpose and design. These considerations all
lead to a narrowing selection of ploys for Blackmarsh's
utility. The one fact that he knew to be in highest veracity,
was the man's ardor for plant and beast; these were the holy
objects of his natural devotion. In this singular observation
could be couched the very key to Blackmarsh's dilemma, he
postulated.

The druid had used a torch at the sacrificial ceremony. Fire is
and was considered a mystical, magical essence or element,
by the superstitious folk. Would the Lieutenant be able to
stealthily lurk in to witness another ceremony and seize the
flame, threatening to burn down the grove? He remembered

his collision with the buccaneers, and his assumed fire strategy onboard the Sea-Dragon. He had not had to utilize the ploy, due to the expedience of the gales. Now, in the enemy's passion for his revered objects of devotion, Blackmarsh could disarm the druid and free the victims to reverse the equation, should there still be any alive. The sum of this operation, would be gain for the Lieutenant, at the cost of his enemy. Considering this to be his chief salvation, he would seek to realize this ploy. Yet, one last question nagged the Englishman. When would the next opportunity arise? An ancillary matter also materialized in his head. He had forgotten about the Sea-Dragon. When he had viewed the camp and the coast before it, he had remembered there being no ship. Had it vanished? Was the anchor pulled up in the night, to allow the vessel to drift away, carried by an errant sea channel?

This disappearance was another mystery to the young officer, as he tried to assay the craft's destiny. Blackmarsh needed more time to educe the causality of the case, but he kept hitting a sea-wall in his path. Time was a precious commodity. To him, in his present need, it was even more precious a commodity, than gold or silver. It was true, both of his plan to defeat the druid, as well as his mission to solve the mystery for the Admiralty. The young-man would simply need to trust that providence would send him the aid he so desperately required. Without fire, he would not be able to obtain purchase over the druid's passion for the plants. If he was denied this trump card, Jeremiah would be forced to resort to a brute force attempt, but under less than favorable odds. Having come to this realization, he morally prepared to face him, man to man, should his primary ploy be dashed upon the rocks, much as a lost vessel in treacherous waters. As the Druid was adamant in his sacred duty and beliefs, so too was Lt. J.A. Blackmarsh in his. He felt the pangs of his allegiance to the Admiralty, to General Wellesley, and to his nation. His actions were dictated by that alliance and duty, much opposite, yet oddly, similar to his present arch-rival and nemesis.

***

Low-tide began to give way to high-tide. The Lieutenant would be forced from the sea-cave once again. He began to return to his observation point above the druid's circle. Progress, as slow as previously, was effected in the same manner. Sporadically, the signalman jutted his head above the grasses and brush to view the encampment, circle, and grove, and to look out over the sea. Once in a commanding position overlooking the coast, he noted the truth of his prior rumination. The Sea-Dragon *had* vanished! He wondered wither had it drifted, if at all?

The journey back to his old spot from the fat-man's squeeze was lengthy, and he finally settled in by what must have been well past High Tea. The druid could be viewed going to and fro, about the circle in the center of his grove. His eyes and hands would often raise to the highest bows of the trees in the grove, where it nearly appeared that he was in conversation with the sturdy plants. His indigo blue had faded, and he began to wash himself from what appeared to be a bowl of the woad in front of him. Was he preparing for a new sacrifice?

Often he would go to the stone altar in the center of the circle, adjacent the fire torch, and lift from the altar a grand conch shell, giving blasts from it, which created a sordid sea-serenade. After this, he would cup his hands about his ears, as if listening to the wind for any muffled signal he might detect. This he did multiple times. In fact, Blackmarsh counted seven times for the repetition of this ritual. The evening sky over the Outer Hebrides had started to fall.

With the darkening of the sky, J.A. Blackmarsh detected a fresh spray of oceanic air sweep the high places of the island. It appeared that the wind was increasing, and a storm would brew that evening. This would be a catastrophe for Jeremiah. His plans would surely wash away, in any gale or tempest. There would be no ceremony, no fire, no opportunity to tempt the wild man with the scorching of his woods. Furthermore, the Lieutenant's lookout in the brush would be fairly exposed to the elements, and he would be prostrate and prone to be buffeted by the fierce winds that would threaten the island.

At his leisure, the giant of a man, swiftly lit the torch, which seems to have been made of rags or sail cloth, which had been wrapped about the pole and dipped into a black, thick, tar-like substance, from a pot he had previously fetched from the cavern. It was a curious operation, observing the meticulousness of his preparations. Was he intent on signaling to someone at sea with the beacon, or was he again overseeing another of his bizarre pagan rituals?

Later, as the winds continued augmenting their force, a large brig suddenly appeared on the horizon, coming from the south. The druid began to stir, and a whirlwind of activity began to unfold in the center of the circle. He erected some kind of pole, which jutted out over the tree-line of his cluster of forest. Anthony peered in be-wonderment, as the druid strung small colored cloth squares to a line, and hauled them up ever higher. It was a semaphore message in code! Blackmarsh eyed the message from his vantage point, but the symbols were oddly blurred. He had studied the colors and the sequence, and did, nevertheless, have a fair guess at what the message read. By his reckoning, the message conveyed "HELP!" Was the ignoble rascal a signalman, after all, just as he himself?

7.

A Bird of a Different Feather

The rays of dawn broke over the crest of the isle, casting its luminosity over the land, which boldly dared to rise out of that bottomless sea of the North Atlantic Ocean. The hunger and fear contained within the bosom of the signalman had induced a mild state of shock, which washed over his conscience, and removed him from the wakefulness of his vigil. He had blacked out due to becoming overwrought at his predicament. The visions of yestereve played havoc with his soft demeanor, and he had succumbed to the desperate stasis of his plight. The poverty of his nourishment had naturally predicated his peril, causing a retreat from the senses. As he slumbered during the early hours and morning of his Hebridean seascape, he had sensed discovery. It was a sensation simulating the notice that his presence had been suddenly observed. But how so? Had he not been masked in the brush of the hillside? Had he moaned in the terror of his stricken and stranded isolation?

Suddenly, and without warning, he was seized upon from behind, by robust, muscular arms, which were wholly indigo blue in color. Once extracted from his hidden post, the blue man roused him to his feet and secured him with twine cords, to prevent his escape. He had become swiftly bound by his unseen, and unobserved assailant. Certainly, he would be jailed by this foe and offered for sacrifice, similar to the other mariners he had witnessed.

The captor led him down the hillside, unable to glance his facial features. Only the indigo blue of the arms and hands were visible to the captive Lieutenant. Shoved and prodded, the captive Blackmarsh was led into the grove. He faced the cave mouth, his back to the sea. From its maw appeared the large man- it was the druid he faced.

"Rory- look who's been a peekin in at aur liddle ceremonies!" said the odd voice.

"Who be ye, I say." said Rory, the approaching painted druid.

"I am an emissary of the Royal Navy, Lieutenant Jeremiah Anthony Blackmarsh. "With whom do I hold the dubious honor of addressing?" said Blackmarsh in a shallow, yet determined breath.

"Midshipman Rory Kegg, formerly of His Majesty's Royal Navy! And now, a redeemed fellow. You are speaking with a priest of nature! An Arch-Druid of the Circle of Water. I commune with the waters, seas, and all denizens therein!"

"You must be mad, Kegg! This bizarre assignation of yours is, but an aberration of purpose and of the mind." replied Jeremiah.

"That be not for you to decide, Lieutenant!" howled the druid.

"Connor, lash this sea-dog to the great oak of the isle! A privy sacrifice to the men of the sea, he shall make!" ordered Rory Kegg, as he returned to his cave.

J.A. Blackmarsh strained his neck to peer at his aft-quarters. It was he! The very same Irish fisherman who had steered him to sail towards Ullapool! What vile treachery! considered the captive Lieutenant. So the helpful Connor was in league with this murderous villain! How had the two collided? And what was the story of Rory Kegg? How had he gone from being a midshipman of the British navy to a piratical killer of crews and men in the Hebrides? It was a mystery to the signalman, who was clearly a bird of a decidedly different feather, than this rogue creature, who had seemingly fulfilled the self-same role of signalman onboard some sundry ship of the line, in the Royal Navy.

As Blackmarsh was hoisted into the tree, he wondered how he could possibly escape, and what sinister plot of evil were these indigo pirates up to? Once hanging in the tree, he could see the others of the crew of the brig, who had been tied and gagged to boot. These hung lifeless from the tree. It was lucky for Blackmarsh, as he had not been gagged. Perhaps he could speak with the traitor and educe his motives for such piratical activity against the merchant fleet of the isles?

The much more important question, here, was posited in the allegiance of the two. What were they up to? What was their motivation for this murderous piratical activity? The Lieutenant was in search of that glue that sealed their coterie together. Perhaps he could use this as a ruse, or as a means for escape or turning his nautical course, which was for Blackmarsh steering towards the grave? Determined to stir the soup a bit, Blackmarsh began to put his theory into motion.

"Matey, call on your co-religionist! I am in want of such an opportunity to send out green shoots!" said the desperate signalman.

"Whot say ye? Ye join weth us?" responded the Irishman.

"Why, yes! Did you not grasp my rage in Oban? To quash the Navy, I mean to do! I'm a fugitive from the law, looking for fresh beginnings with like-minded folk!" defended the Lieutenant.

"Well, I did find you an odd bloke, to say as much. For an Englishman, I mean." said Connor.

"Fetch big Rory! I've a taste to join with you blues! Our fight is with the same foe!" insisted Blackmarsh

"Wait a tic. Don't ye wanders aff mi Kentish Leprechaun!" chuckled the pirate.

Connor returned from the cave mouth with Rory Kegg. The two were washed of the blue, which only trace streaks of showed.

"What is this then? Blackmarsh? Fear for your coming death?" said the giant Kegg.

"I meant to test your waters, like a ship floating into an unknown harbor, I must wean the trusty few! I'm convinced you are genuine now. You see a fugitive in me! I've gone to ground from the Navy. Over the spoilage of the lands of my Kent, no less! I'm a native son of Blackheath. My surname of Blackmarsh is tied to the stark land of my fore-fathers. So many forests felled in my native home; the marsh and heath drained away, and the fauna fled from the naked lands that abide there nowadays. The green has been culled to naught!" explained Jeremiah Anthony.

"What was it ye did to incur their wrath, then; becoming a wanted man?" quizzed the druid.

"I was stationed at Plymouth, in Devon, at the Royal Navy stables therein. When my dander had grown to boiling, I decided to enact my revenge for the cull of Kent's flora and fauna. I loosed the gates, freeing their war-chargers! The beasts flew free of their captivity, and now roam the moors, from Dartmoor to Exmoor! After that, I fled to Wiltshire, to the circle of Avebury to find folk of the druids; alas, I failed. I went, thereafter to Great Stonehenge's circle, but again failed without succor or success." explained the exasperated youth.

"A yarn you spin; most colorful, but is it true, my Englishman?" probed Kegg curiously.

"Be the welkin true and blue, on a bonnie morning?" retorted Blackmarsh.

The druid pondered his captive's sudden turn-about. Was the man lying or speaking with a plain tongue? Jeremiah ever carefully gazed at his visage to read for signs of softening in his demeanor. He was a hard walnut to crack, and betrayed nothing of his feelings to the Lieutenant.

"If you speak with a forked tongue you shall be given over to death; a wee sacrifice. If you speak plainly, you shall be given a chance to prove your words with deed. I, myself, hail from the Isle of Man. I am of the Manx druids. Our circle-the Cronk Meayll- the Mull Hill Circle- be. I sailed with the Navy, by the courtesy of impressment. There I became a signalman for the fleet. A murderous institution is the Royal Navy. Its drunken sailors consume drink and make the ruin of our ancient circle there, in the blind mirth of their firewater. The fleet is a rapier pointed against the land, felling tree and forest, wiping the land clean of leaf, all to build their accursed vessels. From this I, too, fled to seek my revenge on this unholy power. It must be stricken with a hard gauntlet; crushed like a dry husk! Seek you to join us in this cause?" said the Manxman.

"Given a free hand, I shall bring a dagger to close quarters against the ghoulish destroyers! They quash the green under hobnailed boot; they cull the oak, and drain the marsh! Death shall be sated with their corpses, say I!"falsely pontificated the junior officer.

"Compelling, Lt. Blackmarsh, then you accept the test at the Callanish Stones?" queried the druid.

"I accept the terms, wherever these be! For too long have I searched, only to be betrayed by the vazey and perfidious, who have signaled in vain their false druidical leanings." responded the signalman.

"Then, we have a bargain! Release this man Connor. The circle is the better part of a day's walk. We shall depart in the dark of night. You may help our Irishman to rid the great oak of these fetid souls. Feed the soil with their crude bone and flesh! Know this, Blackmarsh, we serve a power greater than you can conceive. Deceive that power and you shall pay heftily, I assure you!" explained Rory Kegg ominously.

"I am prepared to do what is right." calmly explained Jeremiah, rubbing his now sore wrists of their fresh rope-burns.

The two men, Connor and Jeremiah, began lowering the dead crew from the brig, and heaped soil and turf over them in a crevice of the hill. The stony grave received this mortal deposit of bone, blood and leather, in the silence of the Hebridean paysage, with only the whisper of the wind at the men's backs. As Jeremiah Anthony enacted this funerary rite, he secretly prayed for the souls of the men that had been murdered by these dastardly misguided pirates. These renegades had alighted to form their own secret society on the fringes of the realm; an almost chthonian illuminati, these mudlarks enacted their queer amphitheater of the absurd, in the far reaches of these Scottish isles. Blackmarsh pondered how he may put a stop to it. It was clearly *they*, who were responsible for the disappearance of the crews and vessels, the signalman had deemed. What would Jeremiah do to halt this madness? Was he against the odds, or would he triumph against these blue men of the isles?

A meal was given to the young signalman to eat. It was a spartan feast of raw white mushrooms, a salad of clover and greens, dandelion wine, and a dry hard biscuit made of some fibrous wild grain, sprinkled with sea salt. Though he lacked meat and potatoes, the Lieutenant gobbled these down as if he hadn't clapped eyes on sustenance in a fortnight. It certainly was his first substantial meal in many days since the storm. After this was consumed, he was given a handful of roasted pine-nuts, and acorns to masticate, which he effected with a hitherto unknown sense of glee. Several he pocketed to sup on later, should his hunger return.

Blackmarsh mused his predicament once more. He had come to the apparent cause and source of his calling- his mission for the Admiralty. Yet now he was wittingly aiding the very same perpetrators. Upon this fire, in the very same kettle, he had found a signalman, much as himself in training, yet this fellow had turned away from the service because of his own poisoned miasma, plus a sense of victimization at the hands of the Empire. Jeremiah Anthony considered the parallels of his and his foe's provenance. Whereas, Jeremiah had fared well under the auspices of his military experiences, the druid had withdrawn to a realm of phantasms, where the ancient rites of the druids held the primary focus of his being. Kegg cut the figure of a wild, utterly possessed priest of nature, who aimed to punish and thwart, by any means, his native land.

This odd raven of a man, Rory Kegg, had located a kindred soul in his Irish sea-compatriot, Connor, and had gone to ground in the lonely isles of Scotland's farthest periphery.

This druidic coterie, painted themselves in the indigo of the woad-blue, and held bloody rites, yielding offerings of flesh to the sylvan spirits of the isle. The fact that he'd seen to this forest, tending it in the starkest lays of the land, meant that his dedication had been total. Yet, the great oak of the grove was, verily, an ancient sapling of many-fold generations of men. Could he have inherited this, his burden, from an older tradition of the druidic folk? It certainly must have been spawned before he was birthed in the Manx country. Jeremiah paused, considering how he might coax and tease the history of the grove, and, indeed, the gang's activities at the circle of the Callanish Stones, whither the three would advance.

As night began to lower her dark hood abreast the sky of the ocean, the three darkened figures set off for the circle. Rory totted a covered clay pot. Connor packed a small barrel of spirits, by the appearance of the stout little keg. Jeremiah Anthony was saddled with a sack of various mystery rudiments, which dangled and bobbed about inside the deep innards of the burlap bag. During the trek the men spoke in hushed tones. Blackmarsh was able to fathom the relative importance of Connor in the coterie. It was evidently, he, who obtained the provisions for their operations, the main elements of which was Scotch whiskey from Oban. As Blackmarsh had suspected, the druid laced the brew with herbal drugs to incapacitate the sailors, after he had effected a ruse of sorts, either seeking aid or, merely greeting the doomed crews with drink and short-lived mirth. Would the test of the circle be a similar such initiation rite, Jeremiah wondered? Would he be asked to entice some luckless crew of seamen to their dread and doom? This singular rumination sent a chill of banal disquietude into the Lieutenant's inner core.

The foray towards the circle went tediously slow. The lay of the land and was sloping, at times rocky, and brought the men to the narrows of height atop a cliff, which ran in tandem with the coastline. That the group traveled with the sea to their port side, indicated to the signalman a southerly progression. Thus, they were traveling away from the islands northern most extremity. This Blackmarsh also took to mind as they continued their overland roving down the coast of the Isle of Lewis.

After the vanishing of the sun, progress had become even, slower, inching forward at a snail's pace. A single false step would land any would-be adventurer to their demise at the foot of the craggy spine, facing the lonely North Atlantic. Several times, the Lieutenant had foolishly misstepped, which only served to dislodge stones down the drop-off. The others chuckled at this risky footwork, causing Anthony to focus his steps more precisely. His added girth did not aid him in this affair, and he had wished his rotundity was less pronounced on this night. Should he survive the challenge, he would strain to improve his condition, by observing a regime of robust activity. Perhaps, in such a manner, he could shed his belabored burden of Bacchanalian ballast.

Several hours of trekking had brought the men from their coastline roving, to a faintly visible trail, which branched towards a flat small plain. In the distance could be seen ghostly white objects jutting out of the island's crust. It had to be the stone circle, their destination, paused Anthony in his thoughts. The coterie advanced towards the gargantuan blocks of stone in utter silence. The song of the wind was at their backs, and Jeremiah could make out the coastline of the sea in the near distance. As they approached the stones augmented in size and appearance. These were truly enormous, and evidently very ancient.

Once standing outside the circle, the burdens were placed on the ground, and Connor took the sack to hand, which Blackmarsh had been carrying. He untied the sailor's knot at the terminus of the sack, and retrieved a large conch shell, giving this to the Arch-Druid. Connor pulled a large goblet from the sack and placed it upon a stone of the circle, which resembled an altar. He then decanted liquid into the vessel and corked the keg, placing it back on to the earth. The welcoming waft of a fine heather whiskey danced into the nose of the Lieutenant, casting its provenance for all to receive in the olfactory manner. The waft of the potion was vivifying, in the briny sea-breeze.

Now Rory unsealed the clay pot, removed his clothing, and bade the others to attend to their own undressing. Connor explained that the ritual of the indigo wash was the first part of the sacrifice. This, he explained to the Englishman, was part of the purification before offering an immolation to the sea.

Under the light of a crescent moon, the three rubbed themselves of the dye of the pot, acquiring the deep indigo hue of the woad rub. The Lieutenant followed the lead of the others, emulating their holy devotion, to banish any thought he was against their designs; such an eerily odd ritual of worship. He wondered what sort of proof he would be forced to enact to achieve his initiation in to the sect. Would he be pushed to cross a border of personal distaste or moral turpitude, repugnant to the lawful Lieutenant?

Once fully washed, the paint dried quickly. Each of the three was afforded a small handful of berries, nuts, and moist mushrooms to consume. The druid, then, began to chant verses under his breath; these wholly unintelligible to Jeremiah. He then collected the conch-shell, which had been left atop the stone altar-plinth. With this he let escape three blasts of the horn, which rang out over the waves of the great sea. After minutes had passed, the druid repeated the sounding of the shell, with a second trio of blasts. As he blew into the yellow shell, the droning of each sounding was a long, somber reverberation, issuing without echo.

Suddenly and lacking any warning, Blackmarsh ogled the shore, whither the three had been facing. He made out the form of two heads, then torsos, rising from the waters. The dark figures began to close the gap separating them from the circle. As they drew nearer Jeremiah could see their features in the soft moon-light. They were quite dark, as the night itself almost. As he glimpsed them, it appeared to him to be two blackamoors, but as they entered the circle the young officer could espy their features without haze; the pair were blue-skinned men, but by the same token, they were not men. Anthony was faced opposite two stunning blue creatures. He froze as he viewed the creatures of the old legend he had heard in the tavern in Oban- those Blue Men of the Minch!

8.

The Indigo of the Sea

Blue filled the orbs of the young signalman as he gazed at the figures tarrying outside the stone circle. To his starboard, stood the Arch-Druid Kegg, and Connor cloaked in the woad paint. Jeremiah glanced at his hands, rotating his palms to inspect his tint. All five figures bore the same shade of indigo. It was as if the indigo of the sea had covered them in its likeness. At this early hour under a bewitching moon, Jeremiah Anthony Blackmarsh found himself in an explicable moment. The Blue Men stayed outside of the circle, whereas the three men remained within its boundaries. Rory raised the vessel of the whiskey in front of the figures and passed a gulp through his lips of the pottage. He passed this then to Connor, who mirrored the motions. After he had consumed the brew, he too handed the vessel to Blackmarsh. The signalman received the cup and decanted a swig across his lips, swallowing the mixture. It tasted of whiskey, however, a strong herbal additive could be detected in the drink. After quaffing from the cup, he passed this back to Rory, who placed it upon the stone plinth, in the center of the circle.

Jeremiah fixed his gaze to the Kelpie. These had burning eyes of amber, and ropy strands of teal-colored hair flowed from their heads. They seemed to be decorated with kilts of kelp about their waists, and carried man-made instruments of war; knives and a trident. The Lieutenant studied their physiognomy, which was superb and muscular. Their ears were pointed, as well as their noses, which were turned up, rather spritishly. They were bare of feet, and stood upright, as men do. In fact, their appearance was very much in the likeness of men, apart from the skin, which was an indigo blue like that of the sea, and their almost feline amber eyes. So these creatures had spawned the legend of the Blue Men of the Minch. Blackmarsh, nearly in disbelief, wondered what rites of initiation would follow. The young officer's head had begun to swim under the power of the potion, he had drunk.

The chief Storm Kelpie spoke, uttering a language which was unrecognizable as speech. The sound of sploshing, dripping fluids, and surf, echoed in the Lieutenants ears. It was as if the sea was chattering to the men. At this utterance the druid removed a net, bulging with heads, from the great sack Anthony had carried. Upon ogling the bag with his focused eye, Blackmarsh discovered that the heads were not flesh and blood. These were the wooden emblems from ships, chopped from the forecastle of ships the pirates had scuppered. The Irish sub-priest took this net of trophies and approached the Kelpie, proffering it to them on bended knee.

As the island began to heave the roiling of the waves of the sea, Blackmarsh experienced the tumult of a sea-voyage. The mixture was bending his mind, gaining purchase over him, as it inebriated him under its sway. Kegg began to command the Lieutenant.

"Approach them and kneel, Jeremiah!" he ululated stiffly.

The signalman balked at the outset, but felt the prodding of Kegg's strong arm shove him forward. Blackmarsh fell in line with the command, his will diminishing under the spell of the potable, and fell to his knees. At this, his eyes nearly crossed, peered up at the towering water spirit in front of him. He saw the creature handling what appeared to be a sack of seaweed fronds, but it was oddly weaved, and formed a hood. The Kelpie placed this over Blackmarsh's crown and face, and he was encompassed in darkness. The

Blue Men uttered again in their strange bubbly tongue, which issued forth like a babbling brook into the ears of the young officer. He understood he was to stand and exit the circle, which he unwittingly did.

At this he felt the tug of the cold skinned sea-creatures, as they led him down the slope and into the sea. Jeremiah felt the cold water of the sea rise as they descended deeper into the wet wash of the ocean and a darkness overtook the signalman.

***

During the morning of the next day, Jeremiah Anthony awoke in the grove of the druid. The other two were away in the cave, as the sound of toiling bled out of the cavern. What had come to pass during the night? Glancing at his clothes, he could deem that he was covered in seaweed fronds. His clothes smelt heavily of the sea, though, they were dry. He had remembered removing these articles prior to painting himself in the woad. A bizarre notion flitted in to his mind, that he had been taken under the sea, by the Blue Men of the Minch. He recalled the vision of them draping him over with their sea-hood, and he accompanying them into the depths, where he had seen a magnificent underwater city. Blackmarsh was over a whiskey barrel, whether to trust these faint visions. Was it all a delusion of the druid's fabrication, caused by his gathered and accumulated roots, herbs, and potions? Certainly Kegg was able to concoct brews to render men to sleep. Could he have learned to make a nectar of delusion?

Yet, the vision of the Blue Men was vivid to his mind's senses. He recalled the detail of their physiognomy and semblance. Was this then the challenge he had accepted? To alight with the sea-creatures to stand their judgment? That he was back at the druid's bivouac spoke volumes. He had either been conveyed hence by the druidic cult, or he had been conveyed via sea, under the aegis of the Blue Men. Both of these possibilities was frightening to the young officer. He had lost any memory of his return to the grove. Indeed, had he gotten up to anything unsavory under the spell of the whiskey drink and sacrificial food offering, that was consumed, prior to his experience of witnessing the Kelpie-folk?

The signalman stood up, while brushing his clothing of the detritus he had collected during his latest movements about the isle. He peered up the cliff-side towards the druids and then trod up to the cave entrance. Once standing at the entrance, he observed that the two men were shifting whiskey barrels and other supply stores. He addressed Rory and Connor.

"How long have I been kipping here?"

"Ye'd ben lost for tew days, matey! Found ye washed up on the shore thar this mornin!" replied Connor.

"I can't reckon much presently. Only blurry dreams and visions." replied the Lieutenant.

"When you walked from the circle, we saw you headed for the sea with the companions. The guardians of the sea. After you submerged yourself, we knew naught, nor heard naught, till this dawn. You were dragged from the coast and put in the grove to settle." explained Rory.

"Aye, Tha meal at tha table of tha druid's invokes a departur froum tha mynd. When tha fiest iz dooly observed, ett aids one in communing wit tha Kelpie; helps shield from tha fear af tha beasties, an opens tha eears an tha throat, to parlay weth tha blue-folk." continued Connor.

"It is quite a boggle for my brain! That I have been vanished from your company for the span cf two days!" extolled the signalman in amazement.

"You returned to us unharmed. You have been received by the Kelpie, which means you have won them over in some challenge. They wish to commune with you, perhaps they even have a designation for your purpose to them, I thinks." said the Arch-Druid.

"I cannot fathom this business. It is beyond the pale of my senses. It is still unbelievable to me, in truth. I am of the mind that this experience has roots in other quarters. Indeed, the druidic eucharist may have caused such a wild reverie, I consider most likely." hypothesized Lt- Blackmarsh.

The two men laughed heartily and went back to their labors, while chuckling over the Lieutenant's confusion. Jeremiah Anthony plotted his next action. He had, thus far, convinced these scoundrels that he had switched allegiances, but he was becoming pressed for time to effect his mission. If he had, actually, been away for two days, it would add urgency to his task. As he had, by now, concluded without a doubt that the isle where he was situated was Lewis Isle, he began to consider if he could manage to flee the camp during, or just before the fall of night's curtain. Perhaps he could muster succor in the nearby settlement on the island's eastern coastline? Blackmarsh recalled in his study of his map of the Scottish coast a settlement called Stornoway, which was the biggest village on the island. By his calculation, if he be, actually, on the northern part of the island's west coast, the distance could be as far as twenty to thirty miles. Such a gap, would be a full day's trek across rugged terrain. If he were to bolt for the east coast, he would need to put, at least, half a day's distance between himself, and the these druids of the Circle of Water, to ensure escape. Once there, he could present his letter of credentials to the bailiff and request support from the Royal Navy.

As he milled the plan over in his mind, he came to settle on it as his chief hope of scuppering the horror of the druidic circle; and thereby halting their piratical assault on merchants and vessels. The two men were too great in number for him to overwhelm alone. Kegg, himself, was a giant of a man, and his strength gave him the virtue of Goliath-like strength. Perhaps he could drug the men with the same mixture, which they had plied the crewmen with during their assaults? To affect this, Jeremiah would need to deduce the location of its stowage, and secret the admixture into the drink of the men, undetected. This, in its own fashion, would involve a great amount of chance, as Connor had been tasked with maintaining the rations. The signalman needed to assume a burden of trust to gain a closer vantage to the stores.

Jeremiah Anthony wandered back to the cavern where the other two were finishing up their affairs. His movement was loopy, not direct, much as a will-o´-the-wisp drifting from side to side. He still felt recurrent waves of his ecstasy at the circle wash over him as he returned to chat with the broody band.

"I am as a broken oar, of little use currently to the circle. What work may I undertake to augment the common value of our association?" he winced.

"Hmmm…that's a fair query, Blackmarsh. We had pondered about your use in luring the galleys to their doom. You would make for bonnie bate in the enterprise." replied Kegg.

"Aye. Coaxing tha *Sacsannach* vessels to fall for tha ruse af our trap. Always good to hav extra hands for tha haulin of the sacrificial victims." added Connor in agreement.

"That bit goes without saying, but chcres, I mean. Why, I should lend a hand to affairs of the mundane to whit!" defended Anthony.

"We'll give that a think, man. Worry ye not on that score!" replied Rory deftly, curtailing Jeremiah's efforts to get a close look at the supplies in the back antechamber of the cavern.

Thwarted again, Blackmarsh was hindered from a simple resolution to his notion of escape. It was clear that trust was a foundation, only slowly built up, under the careful eyes of the druids. The officer's dilemma again surfaced from the depths. Time was now becoming crucially a factor of the first order of importance. The Lieutenant reconsidered his options. He lacked for the luxury to lounge in the ccmpany of these piratical brigands, loitering indefinitely. The Admiralty had depended on his swift resolution of the affair. Additionally, Admiral Lord Gambier and General Wellesley were, as far as Lt. Blackmarsh knew, still of the mind that the mercantile sea losses had been accrued due to Danish activity. They had observed French imperial naval and diplomatic designs on the harbors of the Dano-Norwegian fleet as part and parcel of the problem, and its possible liaison with these British shipping losses. What if his delay in the affair's resolution were to have a tactical effect on the strategy of the fleet? Such considerations began to goad the signalman to come to a rash decision on the matter.

Escape quickly, he concluded! As soon as he could muster the chance, he must alight. The swifter his action was achieved, the swifter he could deliver the result required by Headquarters. There was little option left for the Lieutenant to maneuver in such limited waters, so to put it tersely. Blackmarsh readied himself to bolt this evening, as the sun was dipping over the western horizon, under the indigo blue waves of the sea.

***

Facing the sea, the three men of this most northerly of druidic circles, sat silently and ate their victuals. These were the same as previously offered. Blackmarsh couldn't help but to think that their sustenance must be terribly bland, and limited to the very same selection nearly constantly. The remoteness of the Outer Hebrides, combined with the clandestine nature of the cult, lent itself to suppressing their visibility to out-landers and islanders, as well. It was only when mimicking distress at sea, or some similar ruse, such as whiskey proffered under a friendly flag, when the duo had made themselves seen to intruders.

Jeremiah masticated his victuals and mused over his impending bolt. Rory and Connor had both labored extensively on shifting the barrels of whiskey, kegs and other stores in the cave. The stowage was quite high due, no doubt, to the multitude of plunder from vessels they had stripped before cutting anchor. The amount of free space for stowage was dwindling, therefore causing the two to re-order the stock to accommodate more for future. When the men would return to the cave after the evening supper to return their meal remnants, mugs, and eating vessels, the young officer could accomplish a small bit of subterfuge to make a dash for the island's crest.

The sun's waning was imminent, and the men had all but finished their evening supping. Jeremiah watched as the men rose to their feet, and headed towards the maw of the cave. A flutter in the welkin caught Jeremiah Anthony's eye as he followed the movement into the branches of the trees of the grove. He became distracted in tracing its location. Suddenly he spied it. It was a small reddish- brown creature. This nestled on a branch high up in the great oak. It was a squirrel, yet, not of the usual variety. The Lieutenant pondered briefly, as he watched the nimble beast sail to another tree. It had stretched its limbs, unfolding like a small ship's sails, and flied to a nearby tree. Blackmarsh was amazed. Surely this beast had found its place here from elsewhere? Perhaps it had come via the agency of a sailor, who had adopted the pet and taken it from foreign shores? From the continent perhaps? An idea came presented itself to the young signalman.

He had still a small ration in hand from his supper, a few roasted pine nuts. These he placed in the center of his palm and extended it to the animal, who had been observing him from his little crow's nest up above. Detecting the scent and availability of the treat, the creature alighted, sailing down from its towering limb above, landing on the arm of the portly Blackmarsh. The tyke was beautiful, furry and wild. As it began to feast on the nuts, Jeremiah seized it with the right hand in one fell swoosh of his hand. He had captured it!

Now, the junior officer was faced with a decision. Should he employ the beast as a hostage to effect his bolt, or proceed to dash the casks of whiskey upon the unsuspecting druids? He had witnessed how Kegg had been gazing often into that very same tree, where the little flier was perched. He had to be aware of its presence. If so he would understand its uniqueness and prominence, having not been discovered prior in these parts. This would hail the beast as of near magical provenance, and import, in the mind of the druid. He could verily count on

Rory's lip-biting and fretting over the thing, should it be placed in peril. Yes, he would stash the little furry rodent into his belt-pouch, as an insurance against the failure of his main strategy of the barrels.

Once he'd secure the pouch on his hip, Blackmarsh darted up the hill. Connor and Rory had entered the cave and were preparing a pot of woad. It seemed that they would hold another ceremony this eve. Strangely they had not mentioned this to Jeremiah, he quickly deemed. They, too, were up to another sordid challenge of initiation, doubtless. Reaching the mouth of the cave, Blackmarsh stood near the last high row of barrels. The druids were hunched over the ingredients of the woad paint, and glanced up in time to witness two barrels tipping upon them. Anthony heaved the pair down from their precarious stacked heights, and footed out of the orifice of the cave. He skirted around the cliff to scale the hill-side. He was headed towards his escape.

On his heels, the wrath of the druids was projected in spiteful bawling and howled recriminations of Blackmarsh's treachery.

As the Lieutenant covered the steep face of the grassy hill, the two had appeared at the bottom and were venting their ferocity. Within the moment Jeremiah heard something whoosh past his ear. A projectile landed to his side. He turned to gauge what artillery was being bombarded upon him. In the blink of an eye, he saw the Irish sailor hurl several small objects at his person. One of these found its target in his shoulder, as Blackmarsh's fleshly limb was pierced. He had been struck by a small dart. His footfalls became steadily heavier and suddenly he was enveloped in darkness.

9.

A Sacrifice in Vain

Lashed again to the large oak, Jeremiah Antony Blackmarsh regained consciousness to find that he was, once more, hanging from the limb of the tree. He was ordained to become the latest sacrifice to this piratical band of sprig priests. Now it was *he*, Blackmarsh, who found himself gnawing his lip. His last plan had gone the way of a soft pumpkin that had fallen from a stone wall; squashed and scattered in to soggy fragments. He was dashed against the rocks of his ultimate failure. All his attempts up to now had been for naught, and seemingly in vain. There was zero hope, even, of securing the fleeting trust of the brigantine-quashing maritime druids of the Circle of Water. Rory addressed Jeremiah in terms of justifiable spleen.

"Ye have been graced with a sea of confidence, offered the olive-branch of the covenant, and yet ye have sinned and connived against it. For this damned misstep, you shall join the Blue Men in sacrifice, as an offering!"

"Sacrifyce be too grand fur dis *Sacsannach!* To Davey Jones' locker with him, says, aiye!" piped up the wrathful Connor.

"You profane God's creation, with violence and blood! It is thee two who have forsaken His covenant! As mudlarks, you shall end your own days, scratching in the muck at the water's boundary!" exclaimed the signalman in high dudgeon.

The druids ignored the curse of the young officer, and merely returned to their designs, namely applying the indigo woad paint to their bodies, setting up of the tar-soaked torch, and washing the ceremonial blades for the evening's blood ritual. Witnessing this misguided mindfulness of the two wilderness zealots, who hungered to vent their crimson rage on the person of the Lieutenant, was a trying ordeal. Jeremiah Anthony, wiggled in his roped bonds, trying to make some form of his last resistance to the fetid conniving of the, now, blue circle men. He strained each instance the two had vanished for an item, or to fetch some material for their enterprise from the cave's deep hollow. With such constant squirming, and at a particular cost in anguish and physical pain, the young officer did effect some splintering of the branch he had been strung to. Effectively, he had started to note the strain of his girth on the thick of the limb. Would he be able to cause its falter under his considerable ballast?

Jeremiah Anthony was portly, corporeal some might even so describe; not to the extent of obesity, yet his girth had certainly been visible to most. The Lieutenant had always maintained that he was constructed of stolid English bones, which had been a healthy and known trait, down his particular family-line. It would be quite the small triumph, should he be able to command that said familial "boniness" to his beck and call. Summoning the sway of the flesh against the grain of the great oak's concentric rings would be a fitting contest to end his days; also with a sense of aplomb it would bring, should he prove able to cleave the limb from the main truck of the sylvan entity. Blackmarsh was decided. He would let fall the girth of his frame to attempt his havoc at the heights of his captivity above.

His thoughts turned to the plight of the fleet and the Admiralty. What was their position, he wondered? Had his errand dragged on too long? Were they already preparing to take measures in hand to counter the French designs on the fleet of the combined Norwegians and Danes? And what were the French currently up to? Napoleon's imperial appetites had burgeoned without bounds since his coronation three years prior. Jeremiah began to drift into his musty recollection of events. Yes. He recalled the coronation. It had been, as he recollected in the thirteenth year of the French revolutionary calendar, in December, or, as they had the odd appellation termed "Frimaire."

Revolutions, Blackmarsh mused, were a murky, cloudy business to be sure. That an entire nation of people should rise up to throw off the yoke of their masters- such masters had got to be utterly distasteful. They could, perhaps, even be down-right scoundrels and tyrants. Was this truly the hurt of Connor and Kegg? Had they rejected British sovereignty and lordship over the isles, out of a sense of tyranny, similarly? Resurrecting the old faith of the Celtic folk was a unique, and to Anthony's mind, singularly rare happenstance. Could it be that there were others on the distant peripheries of the Empire, that shared such common views and aspirations? In the mind of the Lieutenant, the matter had occurred as a sinister affair in utter isolation. Upon this, the druids had communed, whether by design, or by fluke, with the folk of the Blue Men- the Kelpie. This, too, was a curious mystery.

Whence was this union born? Under which auspices had the two sides liaised? On the one hand, the woad-coated priests of wood and water; on the other the indigo-folk of the Kelpie. The semblance of this sea-race was fleeting in the mind of the young signalman. He had been drugged with the exotics of the druidic cult, therefore, his supposed journey under spume and wave had been essentially washed from his recollection. Apart from slight connotations, hints, and faint stabs in the murky waters of his lost adventure, he had no present grounding of the veracity of the legendary visions he had encountered.

In fact, the fables of the Scotch folk had a multiplicity of various mythological and eerie folk-entities. These Anthony had heard sparsely and merely in murmured talk. Such included the newest in his lexicon, the Kelpie, but also, the Brownie, Pixie, Selkie, Shellycoat, Boobrie, Trowie, Tangie, Morag, Nuggle and Boggle. Indeed, to him it verily seemed as if the whole of God's Creation was teeming to the brink with such stealthy, often eerie, and certainly mystical, divers forms spawned by the Creator, or by the very least token, in the rumination of men.

The signalman began to slide into a lurid, nay, garish rêve of these haunting mythical figures, which had begun to fill the Englishman's mind as a glass of limited volume, in the very slops of an over-filled decanter. His heart had pounded, and beads of sweat had dotted his brow, as he experienced an overpowering sensation of fear and doom in one fell swoop. The shade of his eyelids, drawing lower, slowly eclipsed his tiring orbs, as the pangs of his pointless predicament became ever-pressing, prodding him into a black twilight of the safe harbor of the Lieutenant's unfurling unconsciousness. He'd fainted under the duress of the long hour of his unraveling torments.

***

After an unknown quantity of hours, Jeremiah Anthony regained his composure, in that, he was once again restive, having awaken to the sounds of the tinkering of the druidic rabble in the grove. What, if anything, of substance had he missed? Under the solemn shade of his darkened quietude, he had been deprived of the ability to follow the two fellows with his eyes; watching their movements, preparations, and ultimately gauging their soonest intentions. It was in this ignorance of their purpose, that Blackmarsh again stirred anew. The bindings of his arms, lashed firmly to the tree had clearly pained him, and he swam in the ache of those wounds, as well as the pool of impending fear, which bubbled ever more precariously closer to his closing maw. The position was suffocating to the plump junior officer, who had become a tad impatient at the cul-de-sac he had found himself lodged in.

The night had now been waxing steadily, and as the dark dribbled slowly thicker, and nearer his impending doom. Blackmarsh had wiggled at each opportune moment, producing a steady lean to the limb. It had buckled noticeably under his lard and bones since he had last peered over at it. Earlier he had hunkered to make it to do just so. Some occasional popping and snapping of the tree-flesh could sometime be elicited from the wood, adding to the hope in this cause for sabotage by the captive signalman. As this hidden subterfuge took place, the loyal stalwarts of the druid-folk were engaged with their own pious truck. The large conch-shell was carried forth, as well as the holy-book of the Arch-Druid's pious poetical verse.

It had occurred to the young Lieutenant that the affair was going to be made a High Mass rite in their observance to the faith. Such sinister devotions had brought a tide of fear upon the pendulous Blackmarsh. This fear burgeoned after Kegg produced blasts from the oceanic horn of summoning. He was calling the Blue Men to witness this unholy slaughter! Pangs of ignominious dread filled the bosom of the signalman, as a sense of utter failure washed over him. He'd, in the end, it seemed, failed to bring to fruition his first grand charge as a minion of General Wellesley, his own regiment's commander. How he rued the thought of this grand missing of the mark.

Connor looked on approvingly, as the young man wiggled to and fro on the great limb of the tree. He awaited the oncoming of the ceremony. Rory Kegg, too, chanted from his book of penned verses. As the words were intoned by the druid, Blackmarsh had begun to perceive of them as sounding quite silly and rather witless. Jeremiah Anthony caught himself snickering as he drank in the woody verse with his ears. At one point he even began to bray in laughter as he listened to the rot. This action was interpreted as absolutely sacrilegious and, heretical by the fanatical Connor, that he reached for an oaken cudgel and began striking the Lieutenant's feet with the same. At this moment of unfortunate interaction, the Blue Men of the Minch surfaced at the shore, and sauntered up towards the spectacle.

The beating of flesh with the wooden implement caused Blackmarsh to lurch in pain, attempting to dodge the cruel blows of the subordinate Irishman. The Kelpie descended on this pandemonium, with Jeremiah's shrieks and the combative swings of Connor, mouthing loudly with sounds of slurping, sucking, and bubbling, as if a water source was being frantically boiled or reduced by an alchemist in haste. As the junior officer swung on the limb, a sudden and felicitous crack resounded in the ears of all, as the branch departed infamously from the trunk of the oak. It had practically been severed in the process of Jeremiah's fall, bringing the portly man smack onto the ground, with a swathe of the tree's thick bark in tow with the broken branch.

The Kelpie, enraged at this, acted as furious beings. It had seemed to Blackmarsh, after a sudden and indelible notion in his mind, that the great oak was a kindred object to the sea-folk. In fact, he detected a sense of fellowship, or familiar connection with the Storm Kelpie and this king of trees on the dry land. Could he have inherited this idea from his time during the challenge of the hood? It was not at all clear what was transpiring to the Lieutenant, though the wrath of the Blue Men was abundantly evident to all. Kegg suddenly beamed in a gaze of surprise and fear at the developing chaos. Connor, who had by now dropped the cudgel, was on his knees imploring the sea-folk to pardon him. The chief of the Blue Men made his voice fathomable to the druids.

"Foolish men- to have profaned the sacred suck-water entity! Your offering to the sea is in vain! You have soiled the holy offering and destroyed the living relic that dwelt of the circle!"

"Please, lords, it was an unfortunate error!" cried the Arch-Druid.

Attending the Blue chief, his subaltern, wielding a great trident, jabbed it into the flesh of the Irish adept, spearing him like a sea-bass. Connor screamed as he was pulled into the foamy night sea. Kegg, too, implored as the chief seized his great prickly barbed-beard. The master of the Kelpie, swaying the Manx-priest down to the shore, removed a shimmering sea-blade from his side, and plunged it into the heart of the Arch-Druid, bringing the wretch's life to a sudden end.

Blackmarsh was still lashed to the tree's green-wood appendage. As he watched the demise of the men of the circle, he wondered what fate was to fall upon him. He could never have imagined such vengeance from the Kelpie over this transgression of the offering.

The second Blue Man, who had wielded the trident, approached Jeremiah, and lifted him to his feet. They were, now, face to face. Blackmarsh glanced into the amber eyes of the sea-being, and awaited similar punishment. It did not come. The master of the Kelpie, swooshed in the dialect of the race, causing the second to swipe away the ropes of Antony's binding confinement. The chief spoke to the mortal.

"Yours is a heart true in fashion, honorable in design, and worthy of peace." said the teal-haired entity.

"You wish to spare me?" quizzed a puzzled Jeremiah Anthony.

"We have learned of your nature at our first encounter. Ours is a tradition of gentle ways. We seek to ask your aid for a path of common interest and mutual respect. Will you agree to the pact?" said the Chieftain to the youngish officer.

Jeremiah Anthony Blackmarsh was stunned by his ears. What was he hearing? What precisely were the designs of this ancient race of hidden beings, secreted below the lonely waves of Scotland's azure coasts?

The signalman cocked his head up towards the face of the towering Master of the Kelpie. He pursed his lips briefly then, opened his mouth to speak.

10.

Treasure for a Treaty

Words of intrigue had been offered by the mysterious sea-folk. Jeremiah was startled, indeed, he was flabbergasted by the turn of events, only too happy to still breathe the salty air of the ocean.

"Of what aid do you speak? What terms do you seek? I wish to be helpful to your people, as you have shown me the tenderness of fair-bloods. How may I repay this dignity to your kind?" posed the Lieutenant in awe of the Kelpie.

"Command your folk to do the following." said the Storm Kelpie, as he paused to receive the excited signalman's words.

"I am not in such a high place to command, noble one." he explained.

"May you impress our wishes upon your folk?" queried the blue creature.

"That I may. I shall deliver a report to my commander. In it I may relay the terms you desire of men on dry land." he clarified.

"It is acceptable for our purposes." agreed the Storm Kelpie.

"The race of our kind, is of a bygone line. We wish not to be intruded upon. Your kind is filled with irreverent and irrelevant passions, which cloud the pure waters, and dilute our existence and our ways. We ask for serenity in our native waters. When your craft part the waves of our realm, we are perturbed. Therefore, we ask that when you approach us, you hail us with a coin of respect." demanded the Blue Chief.

"This is a humble request, you seek. A farthing for the fathoms. This I can ask to be honored. I shall express this wish to the Admiralty." stated the Lieutenant earnestly.

"Once more, we desire no man to dive the deep of our habitat. Stay away from the deep of these areas from hence to the far side of this land. It is the spawning pool of our race." delineated the Chief.

"You mean this isle here? From the Sea of the Minch around to this point facing the great ocean?" asked Anthony.

"Aye. It is our hereditary zone; this is sufficient to preserve our race. Should your kind wander into our midst, we shall bring death to the perpetrators of the intrusion. We seek solitude, but will not hesitate to raise wave and typhoon upon villainy. Many thousands of years ago, we shared ways with your folk, worshiping in the circles of the islands. We learned the tongue of the seafarers and how to make our thoughts drift into your parlance. The ages ended in failure and exploitation. Since your people thrive on wickedness, we have been forced into seclusion. Your own core spoke to us at the union of our meeting, and we have felt that you may be counted on to press the bargain. As long as we shall receive the treasure, we shall understand your people sail into our pools in peace. Your adherence to this treaty is essential for our safe harbor. Do you consent to the pact?" demanded the Chief Kelpie.

"You have my word as a gentleman of my folk, we shall abide by this treaty. Every vessel sailing through your regal waters shall come bearing a token of this pact. It shall be a farthing; treasure for the deep, and an act of our honoring of the pact. We shall not trod on the sea-beds of your sacred familial pools. This shall remain your own privy palace of the deep." agreed the young man.

"We are grateful that you have come in peace. The others of the tree and water faith, the tender of the great oak and his underling- these promised an appeasement in blood. They were deceivers, and destroyers. Their cores were hidden in lies and deceit, they spoke with forked tongues, and stirred the waters of fear and retribution. With them, they continually promised of impending invasions to our pools, and the need to extirpate the tree-fellers, who live on the dry land, to craft the floating wave-breakers. We agreed to receive their homages, but as you saw, by their unquenchable thirst for blood, they enticed doom upon the Holy Oak of our last circle, and upon themselves." defended the Chieftain.

"Yes, the men had blackest evil in their hearts. They breathed the air of a vengeful brooding, ready to consume men for their own ill passion." submitted Blackmarsh.

"The circles were once maintained across the expanse of seas and the land. This circle, in the nearby cove, is our ultimate circle, and this grove has been tended and replanted over the entire memory of our people. The last sacred oak, has been spoiled by the wicked lust of the those twisted tormentors." said the Blue Man.

"I should be very amused to plant several acorns in the soil here, before I depart away Would it be acceptable to you, to repay this damage, thusly?" asked Jeremiah.

"It shall." replied the Kelpie Master in subtle solace.

"May I ask, of you a kindness, before I return to my people to render this treaty?" inserted the inquisitive young signalman.

"What may this be?" intoned the Chieftain.

"I should relish a small last audience with your people, to show the example of the goodness in my people, so that we are not all thought to be of such crudeness, if you would guide me one last time to glance upon your pleasant realm." inquired Anthony to the leader.

"It shall be so." laconically replied the man of the sea, as he motioned to his lieutenant to bring forth the sea-hood, and place it upon the young signalman.

The Blue Man spoke one last time.

"I should ask you to drop the seeds of the planting at this time. You shall be given an audience in the sea-hall of my folk. You will be attended to and serenaded, as is the custom of my people. After this, you shall be fed symbolically with a morsel of the sea. This is our royal lotus-nectar that we have feasted on since the time of yore. Beings of your folk, the dry-landers, are not accustomed to its potency and you shall become forgetful of what you have witnessed of us, and only be aware of an urgency. Therefore, you shall record for posterity the command of obeisance of the treaty, the treasure-toss to the waters of our realm; however, you should void mentioning the Blue Men. It is the cost we require to maintain our safe harbor. Consent you also to this condition?" stipulated the Master.

"I shall not go counter to your established ways." replied Jeremiah.

At this Lt. Blackmarsh was ushered back to the cave, where he found a clay pot with fresh acorns to plant in the fertile soil of the isle. A fist of pine nuts and acorns, he shoved into his own pocket- this to whet his own appetite or, merely, for his wee delight, later. He also penned, for himself, the main points of the treaty of avoidance of the deep of the waters around Lewis Island, and all ships to lay a coin overboard on crossing the very same waters. When he had completed this entry he tore the page from Rory's druidical tome, and placed it with his gear in the cave.

The acorns were deposited in the center of the grove by fashioning holes in the grassy area with an iron spike he had located in the druid's cave, and dropping an acorn into each cavity. He then filled the exposed holes with loose soil and stamped the ground even with his foot. He was satisfactory that enough berth had been given for the young oaks to rise up to the welkin for the free gifts of solar rays, fresh ocean air, and moist tear-drops of the heavens. Jeremiah fervently hoped that the bonnie dew would greet the deposited hope he had gingerly placed in the bosom of the ground, upholding his goodwill to the Blue Men.

Once these errands had been dispatched with, the young Lieutenant re-joined the Blue Men on the coastline, placing his bodice on the highest rocks over the shore, where the waves were lapping gently and rhythmically with a constant ebb and flow. The subaltern attended to Jeremiah by placing the ready sea-hood atop his crest, and taking him by the hand, led him under the waves. A rush of foamy white water washed past as the trio made their descent to into the flows. A coldness enveloped Jeremiah Anthony as he entered its deep moist. He had not thought about the coldness of the ocean, yet he greeted it in an even stride. The indigo of the upper stratum of waters had been replaced by a darker hue, and by the time the three had touched on the sea-bed, it had adjusted hues to that of a deep violet-black translucence.

The Lieutenant spied the environs nearest him, and could see mantles of crusted stone, sea-plants and fronds were abundant about the bottom of the sea, as well as fishes, clams, and other visible omens of life in the deep of the sea. As the three moved at the bottom, Blackmarsh could detect the presence of dozens of shapes approaching him. It was the others of the Kelpie. Several sat in repose on plinths, and he could very nearly see that he had entered a stone circle of plinths quite similar to the one atop on the land. So these folk had certainly erected these edifices at some time in their long history! He felt a tinge of humbleness seize his frame. The sea-hood had afforded him breathless, effortless sustenance, while in the deep. There was no constraints for him, as if he was breathing air up in the world of men. At the beginning, he was quite taken by this surprise fabrication of the Kelpies' arcane sea wisdom. After a spell he had become accustomed to its function, and natural seeming convenience.

At the terminus of the circle, Anthony was commanded to seat himself on a globular perch next to the throne of the Master of the sea-folk. Dozens of the Kelpie paraded past his vantage point on the edge of the sub-aquatic arena. The features of the water folk seemed to be quite similar, in that each appeared to be mirror apparitions of the others, with a few pronounced exceptions. Certainly the Storm Kelpie Chieftain had spread his progeny wide. The beauty, and serenity of this unspoiled region struck the Lieutenant as an imminent wonder of the world. Had other folk descended on this sacred pool of the Kelpie, there would be bound to be schism eventually, resulting in the ultimate spoilage of the race and of their unique kind. They were surely prudent to take such care to save their realm by warding it from outside dry-landers. Under the poison and the greed of his own race, the noble Kelpie would be starved, ruined, killed and enslaved on the whims of the weak of principle, and conniving of coin, considered Jeremiah.

A female kelpie approached the young signalman, proffering him with a large sea-frond on top of which rested a clam-shell. This was stuffed to over-flowing with a bright-green sponge-like substance, which wiggled in the even movement of the waves. This was the royal sustenance of the sea-people. Jeremiah wonder what it consisted of, and from whence it came? No doubt it, like the sea-hood, was a fabrication of this industrious, but arcane folk. He saw the others consume it in wee handfuls, placed on the tongue and swallowed. The Kelpie's mirth increased as they ate of it. Their eyes gleamed brightly, ever so, and long smiles eclipsed their noble visages.

Now, having observed the manner of the Kelpie, Blackmarsh mimicked the rite and followed in his own suit. He removed a portion and placed it through the fronds of the sea-hood, into his mouth. A salty-sweet flavor of the sea was released into his mouth. Had this been of animal or plant extraction? Perhaps some under-sea mushroom, or the flesh of some soft maritime feast? Anthony was unable to guess at its origin. His own bitter fears and foreboding of the past many days seemed to vanish, as he tucked into the delectable morsel. He continued in this same fashion until he had emptied the entire ration from the now empty shell.

The others grinned at him widely, as he parroted this reciprocally back to the sources. The sea-folk had a serenity, a peacefulness, which begged many questions- were they the mythical origin of the mermaids and merfolk? How long had they endured for in such utter bliss, and from whence had they come? The grace of their race was amply evident to the young man, who felt the goodness of their kind in his very own deepness. The profundity of this aspect was poignant to the Kentish signalman.

Now several females appeared and began dancing in a slow, yet appeasing fashion. The graceful motion of their limbs penetrated Blackmarsh's being, convincing him that the sea-folk could very truly have been angelic beings of the Creator's making, placed in the world to lead the good to their destiny, and the wicked to theirs. Perhaps he was being charmed by the entities? Had they not received the blood sacrifices of the druids? Could their existence be fluid in nature, held in the hands of man? Should a man act in a sinister way, they would not interfere. Should a man be of good heart, they would reward his nobility. In such a fluid manner bending to mirror the ways of men, they had dealt with human interference. In such a light it would not be wise to tangle with their race in a violent or offensive manner, as fire would be met with an even greater fire. It could be that they mirrored the actions of man out of some innate law of nature, that eluded the human grasp, as yet. This was all too much for Blackmarsh to consider, as the substance he had consumed eroded his will to ponder over these loose yarns in his inquisitive nature.

Feeling the gentle tug of the sea-nectar, Jeremiah Anthony Blackmarsh slowly began to fade from his senses. He had become submerged in a sea of contentment and bliss, as the last rumination vanished from his memory.

11.

The Piper's Tune

Jeremiah Anthony Blackmarsh sat facing the shores of the ocean, soaking up its prodigiously damp quality, of that self-same wonder- the North Atlantic. He could recall nothing of his sublime rendez-vous with the Blue Men, nor having even graced his feet by striding about their privy paradise under the waves. Several hours had passed since he had found himself sleeping under the shade of a tree in the grove. His memory had grown foggy, and he had wondered whether it had come to pass that he had struck his head on a fall of some sort, or somehow suffered a blow that had rendered him under the grip of cerebral darkness.

Now, he noted that he had felt himself determinedly peckish. Jeremiah couldn't fathom when he had, in fact, last feasted on his victuals. The Englishman ambled up the hill to the cave and scrounged the barrels, clay-pots, and storage vats for some edible sustenance. He was truly ravished and his insides had rebelled decisively, not in his own favor, needless to say. Ransacking the stuffs, the hungry infantryman had, at-last, located stores to his liking. There was a hidden larder in a pigeon-hole, which was large enough to contain a bread-loaf. Here he fished out a string of salted fish. In accompaniment to the fish-on-string find, were also some cured-meats rolled into a spiral. Blackmarsh couldn't help to think this was not some haul that the Irish Connor had placed for safe-keeping, on a proverbial rainy day? When attempting to regale to himself the manner in which the druids had departed the spot, he had the impression that they had been swept to sea, in an unexpected swell of the indigo waves.

Jeremiah Anthony took to hand the victuals, and poured himself a draft of fine juniper-berry gin from a dusty keg in the corner. This he had spotted victoriously, and to join with this, he took some dried squares of hard Danish crisp-bread, which the piratical druids had somehow collided with, during their reign of terror on Lewis Island. The Lieutenant tucked into the delectables with the unfettered appetite of a Saxon, masticating the crispy biscuits with a generous swig of the dry gin, to wash his palate thoroughly of its desiccated texture. He found a small knife and cut the meat from its spiral into nicely manageable chunks of a size, which afforded an easy bite. This and the dried salted fish, perhaps Atlantic cod, he pulverized rhythmically with his sharp choppers, at one point, biting his own lip, over his overly wanton assault on the feast.

Blackmarsh's focus on the meal was interrupted by a droning sound, approaching from the south. The sound and pitch of the drone blasts grew more and more distinct as the minutes passed. He had heard this old rumble before! The thunder of its voice hurled a flurry of memories back into the mind of the signalman. It was the timber and tune of the pipes! The Highland Pipes, to be sure! "It must be resounding from a passing vessel!" muttered the man to himself. In an instant, Jeremiah jumped to his feet, the fish-on-string swerving wildly about as he maneuvered out of the cave's mouth. It was a ship of the line that approached! Quickly, Blackmarsh scrambled on his weary legs. He must signal them. Glancing about, he moved casks, vats, and crates astray from his path, hunting the premises for the desired cloth squares of his trusty trade.

In a few tics of a pocket-watch, the young officer had homed in on them, much as a homing pigeon. A large crate of semaphore signal flags were spotted in his own petrifying vision, which bordered heavily on that of a gorgon's gaze. The four colored flags were put into the proper order from ascending to descending. He rushed to the pole and strung these to the mast. These moth-eaten old sheets had been employed by the druids to lure crews to the same shore. He raised the signal, much as he had done years ago, in his regiment's service. Rushing back to the cave he peered back into the signals and bunting box, foraging for some other tool that he had seen Rory Kegg utilize. It was at the bottom. A shiny brass nautical telescope. This long skinny device he gathered up and returned to the clearing. Blackmarsh raised the device, retracting its telescopic pole to its maximum extension. Several figures had gathered upon the quarterdeck of the passing vessel. One was clearly fixated on his own position with his own telescope bearing down on Jeremiah. He motioned to another signalman who flashed a mirror at the islander. The Lieutenant answered by indicating to his semaphore "HELP!"

A black-capped officer stood next to these on the quarterdeck, in conversation with the ship's signalmen. Jeremiah Anthony used his own arms to hail rescue once again. As the group of men engaged, from their end onboard, in some deep parlay of the matter, an evident order had been given to the crew. Anthony observed as a landing party was lowered into the bay, and watched them nervously, as they began rowing towards the shore, where he swiftly sprinted to receive them. The four rowers, putting their back into the affair, effected a quick transfer from the hulking war-ship. Blackmarsh was hailed by a naval Lieutenant, who introduced himself has Lt. Parker, of the HMS Glory.

"Lt. Jeremiah Anthony Blackmarsh, on a mission of the highest gravity for Admiral Lord Gambier, the Admiralty and my regimental commander, General Arthur Wellesley!" he bleated.

"Grant him permission to board, oarsman." replied Lt. Parker.

On the way back to the mother-vessel, Glory, Blackmarsh held his tongue in check. He had not wished to reveal the contents of the subject of his mission unduly, figuring that this was privy alone to the Captain, and his cluster of immediate officers, commanding the warship. As the small rowboat came closer to the massive wooden construction, the Kentish signalman couldn't help but size up her firepower. By a brief tally of her port side's armaments, she must have been able to boast a hundred canon. Though he saw by peering over the vessel, and noting its apparent age, which was perhaps twenty or more years, he had reckoned it was a Duke-Class, ship of the line. Very impressive, no doubt, at its ceremonial launch, yet, still today maintaining its tug of respect, mused Jeremiah in awe of its regal and stolid stature.

Once onboard, the Lieutenant escorted him up to the quarterdeck, where the Captain was waiting in attendance, with his second in command. Jeremiah Anthony Blackmarsh withdrew the folded parchment of his orders from its resting place in the bodice and handed it to Captain Taylor, while introducing himself.

"Lt. J.A. Blackmarsh aboard. I've undertaken a matter of the first order of magnitude. My letter from the Admiralty, Commander."

The chief naval officer unfolded his orders and glanced at the parchment nonplussed by its dearth of writing. His dour countenance had betrayed his non-credence to the signalman's claim.

"This paper is awash with streaks, neither legible, nor relevant." replied the senior officer.

Jeremiah recalled his original plunge into the Firth of Lorne, outside the tavern. The document's ink must have been spoiled in that, his first encounter with the sea, not to mention his dipping during the sudden storm, when he had escaped from the brigand's clutches. How could he impress the paper's import and provenance? He pondered briefly before speaking.

"I'd succumbed to the wave, and been thrown in a storm off the Minch. Glance at the bottom; the slight impression can still be recognized, can it not, of the Admiralty's embossing stamp? The wax seal was no doubt lost to the sea in the tempest."

The Commander scanned the bottom of the parchment, registering the ghost of an embossing sign. The mark was barely tangible in the moist sea-breeze of the coastal winds.

"I am supposed to lend credence to this faint impression, lad?" he protested un-decidedly.

"Commander, I've scouted the area, and seen to the dissolution of the mystery of the lost crews plaguing this coast. It is of the utmost urgency my report be sent back to the Admiralty this instance. It is a matter of the most leaden gravitas, and concerns the designs of the French fleet in Copenhagen! Stand you in the way of this sending, or come you to aid my present need?" barked the junior officer at highest of the officers on the Glory.

"What are your requirements and your demands, then?" asked Captain Taylor, seeking a crystalline communication.

"Only passage to Plymouth, and the Admiralty there quartered. What is the date, by the way?"

"To Plymouth I'll grant you passage. We shall turn to aft and sail back to port. As we had hailed from thence, we may resolve this matter there, and amicably I trust. The date is the 11th of August." replied Taylor.

"I pray we are not too much overdue, ere the hour may have waned already." declared the young Lieutenant.

Upon receiving the new direction and destination, the helm changed its course, and began the return voyage with all sails opened to the bluster of the sea-winds. The Glory plowed a hasty channel southward- back to port.

***

Lieutenant Ulysses McDowall sat across from Blackmarsh as he prepared to pen his findings, and actions taken, in his summary of the affair of the lost crews and scuppered vessels. McDowall engaged the fellow Lieutenant with compelling questions, as to his mission. As the second in command, Blackmarsh sensed the freedom to disclose his adventure to the man. By his free admission, McDowall indicated that the Commander had suspected something peculiar stirring in the air, when Jeremiah's semaphore signal was spotted. Blackmarsh's sending had meant that it could only have been relayed by a man trained in such martial discipline. That, in itself, marked Anthony as a possible man of immediate fascination to the Captain. How had he gotten there stranded on the lonely shore of Lewis, for instance, and what was his business this far out in the Hebrides?

The signalman's explanation that he had been hand-selected by General Wellesley to get to the bottom of the mysterious vanishing of crews, and ghost vessels of the merchant fleet, was received by McDowall with a marked modicum of revelation. So this junior officer was in the confidence of such highly placed personages in the service of the His Royal Majesty's Navy? The humble appearance, and non-assuming disposition of comportment Blackmarsh sported, was a sure-fire bit of concealment, which had doubtless, been a prime factor in his appointment to the task by Command. With such a shroud of regularity, and quotidian complacence, the signalman had been assured to sail in, unnoticed by any opposing force, without batting an eyelid. To add to this, his skills of signaling, would, as they had been precisely demonstrated to the officers of HMS Glory, serve as a needed competency, indeed prowess, desirable of such a chosen candidate. It soon became clear to the naval Lieutenant that the Admiralty and Command had been spot-on to choose the man for this mission.

As McDowall fired off his queries to the signalman, Blackmarsh returned each volley with a satisfactory explanation as to the details of his mission. Anthony, sensing an ambiance of mutual estimation, took the Royal Navy man into his full confidence. He even went as far as to request his assistance in the writing of his findings. Ulysses was naturally flattered by this non-presumptive air by his Army counterpart, and made practical suggestions, proffered pointers, and indicated arcane military terminology, which had been lacking in the young officer's official vocabulary in the manifestation of documentary evidence fillings to Command. This rapport, as later years would show, would burgeon into the *largesse* of a successful combination during Blackmarsh's later infantry service in the Spanish Pyrenees; alas, this was as yet unknown to the junior officer, in the face of the man sitting opposite him in the officers' cabinet of HMS Glory. As Blackmarsh and McDowall hashed out the report, the sound of the piper, whose droning bagpipes overhead, could distinctly be discerned. Its charm floated in to the officers' cabinet through a pair of open portholes at the aft of the vessel.

The gist of the chronology of Jeremiah Anthony's summation, as well as the observations, he had made, and the path he had trodden to search out the source of sabotage, and its demise, reflected his travels northward to Oban, where Lt. Blackmarsh had come to investigate the possibility of Danish involvement. He recorded his prime suspect, having been in the stride of his investigation, a one Captain Amundsen, the commander of a mercantile vessel, who had been known to frequent Oban in the procurement stocks of whiskey, with which he sailed back to Scandinavia. The name of the captain's client, Elias-Erik Kaspersen, had also come to the fore as a latent suspect. As the water-level had begun to rise in his observations of the affair, the Danish mercantile presence yielded to another motley crew of brigand suspected in the caper.

Under the sea-power of the brigand's ship, the Sea-Dragon, and under its commander, Captain Evans, the Lieutenant had been promised passage to Ullapool, where, along the way, the captain and crew, robbed and enslaved the Blackmarsh, clapping him "in irons," as it were. Due to the fortunate, or unfortunate, conjuring of a sudden storm in the Sea of the Minch, the vessel was dashed to bits by a sudden typhoon, and Blackmarsh only just managed to elude recapture. This unforeseen event, by the grace of the Almighty, it would seem, or to put it is seaman's language, "mariner's luck," brought him to be shipwrecked on Lewis Island.

Once there, he was able to witness the capture and scuttle of ships of the merchant fleet, as well as the piratical murder of the crews, and plunder of the stocks onboard. Injured and fatigued from his near-drowning, the Lieutenant managed to hide away from the pirates of the far shore, where the band had camped out and lured ships and crews to their demise. The ring-leader of these pirates, and man chiefly responsible for this sinister evil, was, himself, a former signalman of the Royal Navy, Midshipman Rory Kegg. He was assisted in this misguided venture by the help of an Irishman hailing from the northern coast of the Emerald Isle, known to the junior officer only as "Connor." During the stride of his observation of their illegal activities Lt. Blackmarsh was captured and threatened with death by hanging. As a result of the strain of his own meaty frame against the natural grain of the oak, the limb was rended from the tree, allowing for Blackmarsh to attempt an escape. During the abolition of his slavery to the great oak tree in the pirates' camp, the Lieutenant freely admitted he had lost much of his recollection of the struggle with the pirates, who had, to his foggy recollection, been passing themselves as acolytes of a lost druidical cult of the stone circle of the island. In the conflict with these mudlarks, J.A. Blackmarsh's intuitive notion of the events painted the picture of a struggle on the shore of the island, where an insurmountable indigo tide of the sea had swept up and washed the two miscreants away-back into the spume of its white crests. He, himself, was taken under briefly, by some odd undertow in the current of the bay. Subsequently he found himself ejected from the waters back to dry-land. The struggle had been valiant, treacherous, and a last test of the young signalman, in the stride of which he received a sudden smack to his cerebrum on the rocks on-or-near the water's edge. The aftermath of this battle on the coast, and bluish sea-swell, was that the Lieutenant found himself washed up on the shore, alone and ridden from the unpalatable company of the sinister duo. No more ships, nor their gallant crews would be sacrificed to this insidious coterie in the Outer Hebrides.

Ulysses' hearing of this tale of the North was one of fascination, and lent him the notion that Lt. Blackmarsh had been a resourceful scout and investigator, having survived nearly three weeks, in such bleak conditions, of undernourishment, captivity, conflict and melee with his co-combatants. It was a miracle that, alone, he had so favorably fared in his faraway feats!

The report, worded, re-read, and re-written in immaculate strokes with a proper goose-quill feather and dark black ink of oak-galls, was rolled up into a tight scroll, after his signing and stamping, and sealed in wax with a signet from the ship's cabinet. This would be handed over once the Glory was docked at shore in Plymouth. With the official notes concluded, Lt. McDowall poured a crystal goblet of dry Spanish sherry for the hungry Blackmarsh, and fetched him a platter of victuals to feast on.

"Spoils from Trafalgar, that wonderful red; or at least, so I am told!" said Ulysses jocularly.

***

Anthony was roused from his temporary quarters on HMS Glory by the sound of the piper working over his mirthful chanter. The drones were releasing the ghosts of a melody. It had begun firing up like a great dragon warming its breath. Then, the artful piper began to play fluidly. It was a march of some kind. Lt. McDowall came in to announce that the officers would be dining soon, and inquired whether Blackmarsh wished to be in attendance as this would be the last meal shared together before reaching landfall in Plymouth. Though this was only a soup course, Blackmarsh took his bodice into hand and joined the other officers at table. One of these mentioned that for the entertainment of the officers and their army guest, and to aid their digestion, the piper would be playing fine martial music, most central to which would be *"Sprigs of laurel for Admiral Nelson."* This swiftly effected a hasty cheer from the men, who were quite evidently very fond of the tune!

12.

A Message Well Received

Plymouth harbor seemed the penultimate hive of activity to young Lieutenant Blackmarsh, having experienced only the harbors of London to be even more frantic, and teeming with all sorts of movements of men, craft, and beast, embarking, disembarking, and meandering the quays of the busy hub. As the HMS Glory had dropped anchor, Jeremiah's anxiety rose to its ultimate climax. Would he be in time to report his findings? Several vessels were clearly being laden for some enterprise of substance. Were these to counter the French sea menace in the Baltic or elsewhere, he pondered?

Captain Taylor bid the Lieutenant adieu and sent his second in command, Lt. McDowall, to accompany the signalman to the buildings of the Admiralty. Perhaps he had wished some form of confirmation that the young officer had, indeed, been on the orders of Headquarters? In any event, he had complied with Blackmarsh's transport, which, in itself was a fortunate factor in the junior officer's swift materialization at Plymouth harbor. Ulysses walked in lock-step with Jeremiah Anthony as they walked in to the chief administration cabinet.

The two men were greeted by a civilian clark, who after gathering the pair's principle cause of presence, proceeded to usher them into the bureau of a secretary, serving at the Admiralty. After a quarter of an hour the secretary appeared and led the pair of lieutenants into a meeting cabinet, where the two were seated in attendance of their reception by Command. Butterflies burgeoned in Blackmarsh's belly, as he belabored the moment of his reception. He had hoped the mission summary would be sufficient, and helpful to Headquarters, and his results taken to heart. The endeavor had been his first stab at such a task, and even with the considerable assistance of McDowall, the lurk of fear was still ever-present in the pit of his stomach.

As he waited the arrival of his host, Jeremiah's mind reverted to the odyssey he had only just returned from. It had been a blow to his frame, a strain on his vigor and constitution, and had bred constant terrors to his troubled mind, as he swam in the fear of his predicaments. He had frequently hungered, been saddled with worry, suffered the infliction of substantial bodily hurts and discomforts, and been subjected to abject imprisonment and the woe of uncertainty it entails. Now that this had all been finished, an Atlantean weight had been removed from his person. His demeanor suddenly softened. A feeling of a relatively relaxed repose swiftly washed over him. The butterflies in his gut were preferable companions to that of the trials of his recent Scottish errand!

The double-doors to the cabinet were briskly parted, allowing the hosts to file into the room. Present were Jeremiah's own commander, General Wellesley, Admiral Lord Gambier, an adjutant to the Admiral, and two other high officers of the Admiralty staff. The two lieutenants immediately rose to their feet upon their entry, giving salutes to the senior rank, in observance of military protocol. Wellesley spoke first, in addressing the pair.

"It seems you've completed your virginal errand, Lt. Blackmarsh. On this I congratulate you personally. Please present your findings."

"Admiral, General, and assembled officers- you may rest assured that the menace of the Minch is finally resolved. I present to you my summary report in this sealed document, for your privy perusal. The traitors, who instigated this sabotage have been thwarted, and no longer breathe the free airs of the British Empire." relayed Jeremiah Anthony in astute language.

"Is that so, Lieutenant? And the involvement of the Danes, the French?" questioned the Admiral.

"A line of inquiry pointing to the Danes was followed up and eliminated in the stride of the investigation. Their neutrality in Scottish waters, appears to be maintained." replied Blackmarsh.

"Tactical deductions will be made and drawn by Admiralty, Lieutenant." retorted Gambier, as he unscrolled Blackmarsh's report.

A blush of discomfiture from overstepping his station washed over the face of the junior man. Would his data be ditched as bilge-water from the bottom of a ship of the line, or savored and gleaned for import to Headquarters? As Jeremiah fretted over his reception, Gambier read through the report attentively. After he had finished it, he passed to to Wellesley for his review. While Anthony's commander was engrossed in the letter, the Admiral snapped his fingers, at which an attendant appeared with a decanter of port and a small colony of crystal goblets on a silver service. He placed this on the long oaken table of the cabinet, and decanted drinks, handing these to the pair of junior officers.

"Drink, gentleman." said the Admiral with a balanced semblance.

General Wellesley completed his study of the paper, and rolled up the report, handing it to his adjutant. He picked up a goblet and joined the others, as the Admiral was handed the same.

"You've collated your finds and reported superbly, Lieutenant. That you have snaked out the villains is to be lauded in the highest terms of praise. It is an unmitigated success. My gratitude to you, Blackmarsh." said the General.

"Thank you, Commander. I should make a small request to honor all of the crews whose lives were taken in vain by the pirates. The idea of a noble gesture to remember their sacrifice fell upon me, a gift of angelic rumination. Would it be untoward to request that all vessels passing through the Sea of the Minch and the far side of Lewis Isle toss a farthing to the depths, in their remembrance? As a murky graveyard, it should, likewise, be left undisturbed by human prodding of the funerary zone." said Anthony.

"That is an immaculate suggestion, and worthy of the sailors of Britain's navy and merchant marine. I see no reason why not. Adjutant, please make a note of that, and issue an order to the effect, forthwith. We are content to hear that foreign elements were not to be found to be involved in this nefariousness in our northern waters. This, however, does not stay our hand in the need to arrange matters of current political urgency." stated Gambier.

"Yes. It has been decided to neutralize the Danish fleet all the same. Their existence is, at present, like sharp trident, which may be wielded at anytime against the throat of the Empire. A veritable Damocles weapon, pointed at the jugular! We've already dispatched elements of the fleet, and Lieutenant, the regiment, too, shall sail to tend to the business." explained Wellesley.

"Ah, I see. Yes, it is unavoidable. The French despot leaves little room for trust, it must be agreed by all." replied Jeremiah in comprehension of the philosophy for this action.

"We are boarding our ships tonight. We sail to bombard Copenhagen, to seize or scupper the Danish fleet. It would be magnanimous to your service, should you choose to join the regiment, despite your recent adventures. Are you game for it, man?" remarked the General.

"I shall be honored to do so, Commander. Who may scry what singular obstacle awaits or what sinister brume may cloud the eye of our endeavors on those distant shores? Please count me in." declared Anthony, full of the zeal of youth, a tad drunk with his message well received by the Admiralty.

Ulysses, who had spent the entire time silently observing this unique spectacle, sipped from his goblet taking only small swigs. This was all rather impressive to him, and he felt grounded in his duty, that the Glory had conveyed the signalman back to Plymouth, without failure to heed the message. Should that have come to pass, a loss would surely have been accrued, due to their failure to follow through with aiding in the report's dispatch.

As the men continued with some additional words of congratulations and predictions as to the Scandinavian Campaign, a sudden and untoward movement was detected on Jeremiah Anthony's person. The Admiral indicated that the young officer's clothing appeared to exhibit the air of a haunting of some unseen activity.

Blackmarsh peered down at his pocket and released its purchase of the clasp. A small furry head jutted out, ogling the cabinet and those present with lilliputian black eyes. It was the creature he had pocketed all those days ago in the grove! Apparently it had feasted on the fist full of pine-nuts and acorns he had shoved in for his later dinner. The officers were a bit taken by the surprise.

"Hallo, hallo!" declared Gambier.

"Quite!" said Wellesley in awe.

"Your report said nothing of an ally on your adventure, Blackmarsh!" said the Admiral in a humorous vein.

"Oh, this squirrel, yes. I nearly forgot the fellow. Seems to have been eating and sleeping in their for quite a spell! It can fly, you know- very rare! Found him in the grove of the enemy of the Minch!" explained Jeremiah.

"A rarity and flies, indeed! Speaking of the Minch, Blackmarsh, it is a reputedly remote and mysterious place in the legends of the Scotch folk." ejaculated the Admiral.

"That it certainly be!" said McDowall, finally breaking his self-imposed silence.

"Lieutenant, while traveling those parts of the sea, you didn't, by any chance encounter the Blue Men of the Minch of local legend? inquired Admiral Lord Gambier with a tinge of fabled curiosity.

"Did I encounter the Blue what? queried the signalman suddenly, in utter misconstruction.

<u>Books and Blogs by the Author</u>

Tea & Espionage: Tales of a British Diplomat 1892-1912

The Un-Natural Case of the Leadenhall Interlocution League

Betwixt Vexes: The Secret of Mordaunt House

The Sinister Affair of the Blue Men

The Monster of Zaragoza
(Coming in Fall 2020)

Tea & Spirits: Quatrains at Seven
(Coming in Summer 2021)

https://teaandespionage.wordpress.com/